THE SURF DETECTIVE

Michael Conway

Conway, Michael
The Surf Detective
ISBN 978-0-615-41214-6

First published in 2011 by
Michael Conway Publishing
PO Box 230413
Encinitas, CA 92023
thesurfdetective@gmail.com

Cover by Mike Conway, Mary Conway, Chandra Conway and E. Martin

Thanks to my editor, Chandra Conway, for her hard work and to Jeff Archer for all his help.

Additional copies of this book available at www.amazon.com, www.barnesandnoble.com. Also available in e-format.

In memory of Daley Dog Conway

Chapter 1

MORNING FIX

I stood on the cliff above the white sandy beach and, looking out over the flat Pacific Ocean, I thought about how stupid I am for loving a sport over which I have no control. The fact is surfers are completely dependent upon Mother Nature to provide waves. And when surf-less days stretch into weeks, the withdrawal intensifies and becomes the itch of a nasty dry spell. I sighed loudly and muttered a few choice words — the surfer's curse strikes again.

No waves meant I'd have to go with option number two for the day ahead: work ... just as soon as I finished my coffee.

Each morning, I'm awake by 5:30. First, I descend on the coffee maker. Then, I turn on the Weather Channel. Usually, the light of day is still spreading over the small coastal town of Encinitas as I make the two-minute drive to the beach, passing by my office on the way. I've been a general contractor for almost as long as I've been a surfer so the early wake up is habitual — even when real estate, construction and the housing market are flatter than the surf.

Behind me, a car pulled up to the overlook. "Here comes the second sucker of the day," I thought. "He'll find no fix here for his surfing addiction."

"Hey, Mike."

I turned to see Paul Maguire, owner of White Sand Surf Clothing. Paul is just one of the very successful surf entrepreneurs who calls Encinitas home. His silver BMW

X5 glistened next to my dusty work truck, better known as my rolling toolbox.

"Hey, you should've called first, I could've saved you the trip."I motioned towards the water with a thumbs-down.

Paul laughed. "Yeah, I know. It's been flat for days."

We shook hands and assumed the position of bay-watching. Paul and I have known each other for several years socially and professionally: I was the general contractor on his custom home. If I'm still on good terms with someone after the stress and strain of a construction project, I call that person a friend.

"Actually, I wanted to talk to you, Mike. I have a favor to ask."

"You need me to build you another house?"

I expected to get another laugh out of him but Paul's expression was serious. "No, listen, I'm hoping you'll track down Bobby for me. He took off the night before last and hasn't answered his phone since."

Bobby Contraras is a young talented surfer who likes to party but doesn't know how to keep a handle on it. His drinking and drug use got pretty bad about a year ago but since then he's cleaned up and he's been working steadily towards a world surfing title. We make for odd friends, Bobby — a 23-year-old whose regular morning snack after surfing is a carne-asada-and-French-fry burrito — and me, an older, stocky, blond-haired dude who's started counting calories.

I'm cool with being a father figure if that's what Bobby's looking for but my message to him is the same one I give all the kids at the beach: "Stay away from drugs and alcohol and keep surfing." But, in the end, it's up to them. I'm nobody's babysitter and I had no desire to peel a hung-over Bobby off someone's couch for Paul's benefit.

I knew one of the main reasons Paul was looking for Bobby was because he was the most successful surf team member. Each year, professional surfing holds a series of 12 contests at locations around the world. Points are awarded according to a surfer's placement in each contest. With two contests remaining this year, Bobby is ranked number three. I wondered how much White Sand's market share stands to gain if Bobby becomes the world's number-one surfer.

When I started surfing, the most you could expect if you were really good was a free surfboard and maybe some T-shirts. The sport has grown from a bunch of guys shaping boards in garages to the point where top surfers make millions in clothing, shoe and surf equipment endorsements.

Paul must have picked up on my energy because he changed his approach. He said Bobby's sister, Maria, was seriously worried about her brother's whereabouts.

Maria is Bobby's only family. Shortly after Bobby was born, his father deserted the family. His mom died when he was still in grade school. Maria is older than Bobby and keeps her eye on him as best she can. She loves him and wants the best for him and encourages him to make the most of the opportunities that professional surfing has to offer.

"Bobby came by her house on Wednesday afternoon," Paul said. "He was drinking, but he was mellow. Later on, Ramon showed up and before Maria knew it, they took off together. She hasn't heard from him since and neither have I. He missed a team meeting yesterday."

During the short time we'd been talking, the Blackberry in Paul's hand had chimed several times. He stopped for a second to look at the messages and then continued. "You know Ramon?"

"Yeah. Ramon doesn't surf."

Ramon is kind of a drifter. Nice enough guy, I guess, but steadily unemployed and just a little ... off. One of those dudes who seems to know everyone and everyone seems to know him except he doesn't really know anyone and no one really knows him.

"That's the thing, Mike. He's not Bobby's party crew. Plus, Bobby's really been buckled down the past six months, living at my house and staying very focused on the title. It doesn't make sense from any angle, really. Maria's scared. She's really disappointed that he's drinking but if he starts doing drugs again, it'll all get out of control quick. She asked me to ask you to find him, Mike. She trusts you and he trusts you. He won't put up a fight with you."

He put his phone in his pocket, folded his arms over his chest and looked at me. I looked back. Paul is average height, I'd say, and a little overweight but not fat. To me, he looks like an English country squire, totally non-threatening. That said, I've heard how sharp his tongue can be — he knows how to cut to the chase.

"Plus, you're low profile, Mike. I don't want to make a big story out of this. If Bobby's back to drugs, I need to get him turned around ASAP. The G-land contest is right around the corner."

"Well, if I agree to track him down, where do you think I should start?"

"Try Caesar," Paul said. "He's Ramon's cousin. Caesar's been spending a lot of time at the migrant camp by my house or he'll be hanging at one of the local parks."

While Ramon can be called a drifter, Caesar could well be the definition of a homeless guy. The situation was weird, I decided, and I was a little worried.

"Yeah, I know Caesar. I'll see what I can find out."

"Awesome. Thanks." Paul grinned and slapped me on the shoulder; he was relieved, I'm sure that he'd found someone to do his dirty work.

* * * * *

My office is located one block from the beach, in downtown Encinitas. Southern California's Old Historic Coast Highway 101 runs north and south through downtown, which is just about a mile's worth of a business district. Highway 101 was the original route that connected Los Angeles to San Diego, but the bulk of that traffic moved to the Interstate 5 freeway when it was constructed in the mid-1960s. My office is in an old two-story stucco building in the heart of downtown that houses the bus station and retail shops on the street level and offices upstairs.

The gift shop does double duty as the local depot for buses running between L.A. and San Diego. The buses bring a regularly scheduled burst of energy to the building's large lobby as passengers pick up snacks and magazines from the gift shop and chat on their phones while they stretch their legs. In between arrivals, though, there might only be one or two people sitting among the several rows of seats in the waiting area.

Before I went up to my office, I stopped into the gift shop to say good morning to Claudia, who works the day shift and takes messages for me and other odds and ends as the needs arise. Claudia is a pert little brunette with some seriously big tattoos on her arms and a tiny diamond earring in her nose. She doesn't pull any punches and can be relied upon to pick up, and relay, the unspoken parts of a conversation.

I told Claudia that I was looking for Caesar. "Sure, I'll let you know if he comes trolling," she said with a laugh. Distracted travelers sometimes leave items behind in the depot waiting area and Caesar regularly breezes through in the morning to see if he can pick up a book or a scarf for himself before the building's security guard collects them.

While my office is small, it's a corner space with windows that overlook the four-lane Highway 101. From my desk I can see the cars and foot traffic from two angles and some days I put my feet up and study the action for longer than I like to admit. But, I've been known to do some of my best problem solving while staring out my office windows.

The view also reminds me how thankful I am that I don't have to commute to work. There's something about being insulated and encased in a protective metal enclosure that causes normally sane and mild-mannered people to turn into horn-honking, finger-flipping maniacs when they're driving during rush hour. I know these very same people don't act that way once they arrive at work.

Work. Right. I resigned myself to a rather nasty-looking set of house plans that had been waiting for my attention. After 20-plus years as a general contractor, I still have a tendency to procrastinate when I'm faced with putting a bid together for building a custom home. Pricing out a house is a very time-consuming process and, at the end of the day, there's no guarantee you'll get the job. It may take a plumber or electrician several hours to do an estimate, but a general contractor has to provide a price for the entire house. It can easily take weeks to gather all the various costs.

Construction is a stressful business. There's the constant pressure of time and money and on some days, one disaster just seems to follow another. Consequently, I've developed a very "thick skin." Or maybe it's just that my nervous system has been deadened by over-stimulation because I rarely get over-excited or raise my voice and it takes a great deal to cause me to lose my temper. Whatever the reason, it's a good thing because to complete a project, a general contractor must be able to work with all sorts of personalities. In the course of an average workday on a job site I may have to speak to an "all-knowing" engineer, architect or building inspector one minute and then turn around and talk to a newly-released felon who's erecting scaffolding. (It's almost a cliche, when reading a crime story in the newspaper, to find the suspect described as an "unemployed construction worker.") The fun never stops in construction so I've been forced to develop my people skills along the way.

When Paul Maguire first contacted me about building his house, I hesitated, because I'd heard some bad rumors about doing business with him. In construction, there are only two types of people; those who pay their bills and those who don't. After meeting with him, I decided to give him a chance and in all our dealings he'd been fair and open, seemingly a straight shooter. Still, during the construction of Paul's house, I encountered sub-contractors who turned down bidding on the job because of bad experiences working with him.

Eventually, I decided Paul can be quite demanding and if he thinks he's in the "right" on an issue, he won't compromise and consequently, he makes enemies. But he can also be extremely personable and generous with his friends and business acquaintances he trusts. Paul is hard to figure, he has a kind of "Dr. Jekyll and Mr. Hyde" personality and seems to make either enemies or friends.

After putting in a couple of hours with the house bid, and with no sign of Caesar, I took a break and drove out to Paul's house in Olivenhain Canyon, a rural community about five miles inland. On the way, I cruised by a couple of the local parks to see if Caesar was hanging out, but no luck.

Paul lives near the end of a private road that meanders up into dusty-brown hills. The homes are large and the styles vary but the yards are all similarly blanketed with perfect green grass or lined with orange trees. Paul's house is a split-level modern design. The lower level cuts into the hillside, while the second floor is full of windows and several decks take advantage of the views toward the ocean. When I got out of the car I was met with quiet, which is unusual because Paul runs portions of his business from home and there are always people around. Bobby's car wasn't in the adjacent parking area.

I took the walkway from the driveway to the lower level patio. The French doors weren't locked so I opened them and gave a shout.

"Hello!"

I walked into the family room and across to a reflecting pool that sits at the base of a two-story indoor waterfall. Bobby stores his boards next to the pool but I couldn't tell if any were missing.

"Hey, hello! Anybody home?"

I walked back outside, closing the doors behind me. Using the stairs off the patio, I started down the hillside toward the migrant worker camp where Paul said I might locate Caesar. At the bottom of the hill, I took a narrow trail that led me into the ravine where I found a small flat clearing surrounded by scrub oak and chaparral.

I've read that in San Diego County there are 7,000 homeless agricultural workers and day laborers. It's hard to say if that statistic is accurate but I do know that for as long as anyone can remember there have been groups of workers living outdoors, whether it's next to a highway or in a canyon next to a well-to-do neighborhood. There are a lot of opinions and issues swirling around undocumented migrant workers but no matter where you stand, it's pretty mind-blowing that in the U.S. there are people living under bushes within walking distance to million-dollar homes.

In the clearing sat three small structures. They were tents, really, but bolstered with some blue plastic sheeting here and a plywood wall there. Regardless of what they

14

looked like I still felt like I'd just walked into someone's living room unannounced so I was cautious and edgy as I looked around. I cleared my throat and was about to announce myself when the cover flap of one of the structures opened and Javier stepped out.

"Hey, Javier. What's up?"

"Not much, slow day today. How are you?"

Javier is a local character who runs a popular gardening service and is known around town as "Javier The Gardener."

"Ah, I was up at the big house looking for Bobby Contraras but no one was home. You haven't seen him have you?"

"I saw Bobby a couple of days ago ..."

"Wednesday?"

"Yeah, that sounds right."

"Do you know Caesar's cousin, Ramon? Was he around, too?"

"Yeah, both those guys were here, Caesar too, drinking with us around the fire. Bobby and Ramon took off late for Ensenada, said they were going to the San Miguel Surf Contest. Ramon was going to see his family down there, too."

"Did Bobby seem okay? He's not answering his phone and his sister is worried. That's why I'm looking for him."

"Well, by the time they left they were feeling no pain. They were both putting away the cervezas and hitting on the Tequila pretty damn quick."

On the drive home, I called Paul with the news that Bobby had headed south of the border.

He wasn't happy. "Bobby must have been drunk on his ass to pull a stunt like this without telling me first."

"Sounds like he probably lost his phone and I bet Ramon doesn't have one so that's why Bobby hasn't been in touch."

"The kid has been so focused. It doesn't make sense for him to take off for so long. He went down there Wednesday night. The San Miguel contest doesn't start until Saturday. No, either he's on a bender or something's happened and he's stranded. Either way, I need you to go get him."

"Well — ."

"Listen, Mike, I don't know if this a big deal or not but I can't wait to find out. I'm thinking about Bobby's career and trying to cover all our asses. I've got deals in the works that require him to stay clean. If you go down and find Bobby now, then if need be I can keep whatever he's gotten into quiet within the industry. Otherwise, if he shows up at San Miguel for the contest tomorrow and he's wrecked, then all I've got is damage control."

He barely took a breath. "Once you've got Bobby and you can keep an eye on him you don't have to hurry back. Get yourself some surf. Hey, and take your buddy Wayne with you. He'd be good to have along. Everything on me, of course, all expenses paid."

* * * * *

Wayne Kozniak is my friend, surf bro, sometime employee and confidant. We've known each other since our earliest days at the beach. I called him after I got back to the office and he was all for the rider-pick-up-followed-by-surf mission. We agreed to meet at the office at 2:00 p.m. so we could try to make it past the border just before rush hour.

I also called Maria Contraras. She was confused but appreciative. "This is so not like him, he always checks in. His phone is going straight to voicemail."

"Don't worry, I'm sure he's just blowing off a little steam. You know, the pressure of being so close to wrapping up the title is probably getting to him."

"I hope that's all it is, but I'm so glad you're going down there, Mike. Thank you. And thank Wayne for me, too."

After I hung up with Maria, I was feeling like I was the one who needed reassurance. I had next to no information on Bobby's whereabouts and Paul wanted to keep quiet the fact that I was even looking for him. I had to try and talk with Caesar before things went any further.

I first met Caesar when I was much younger and working a part-time summer job for the County Department of Parks and Recreation. My duties included daily rounds of all the local parks to do maintenance, gardening and cleanup. It didn't take long for me to figure out that Caesar and his cohorts were among the local coastal homeless population who were "camping out." Unlike some of the other park denizens, Caesar was always pleasant, respectful and most importantly, he cleaned-up after himself. Gradually, we started talking and I was surprised to discover that Caesar, "the bum," was educated and intelligent. He told me he had a family and a job but that he had given up that life to spend his days, in his words, "as a man of leisure and a connoisseur of the finer things in life."

All these years later, I figured I'd try him at one of his favorite roadside parks and indeed, when I pulled up he was holding court with two of his cronies at a picnic table under a huge California Cypress. I greeted him in my usual way: "Caesar, what's *haaappening*?"

"Hey, Miguel."

"So, I need some info on Ramon and Bobby. You know how they took off to Ensenada? Well, I promised Bobby's sister that I'd go down and pick him up. Only I don't know where they're at and I think Bobby lost his phone so I can't call him. Can you help?"

"Ramon doesn't have a cell phone."

"Yeah, I figured."

"I know Ramon was going to visit his parents. That boy misses his mama."

"Do you have a number for them?"

"Nah, I don't even think they have a phone. They live out in the sticks. But go see my other cousin, Eduardo, when you get into town. Tell him crazy Caesar from Encinitas sent you. It's a little joke we have. Guaranteed Ramon and Bobby hooked up with Eduardo and he'll point you in the right direction. He works the door at Hussongs Cantina in Ensenada. You know where that is?"

"Everybody knows where Hussongs is."

"He can tell you where the family's house is at — my memory isn't what it used to be. And don't worry, he doesn't like to let people know, but his English is as good as mine."

"Okay, thanks. Can you think of anything else they said about the trip before they left? I mean, I didn't even know those guys were friends."

"Yeah, they're a strange pair."

Caesar got up from the table and stretched. He'd probably been sitting in that spot since he had his morning coffee at the 7-11 across the street.

He motioned for us to walk and then started talking again when we got a few feet away from his buddies. "All I know is they started talking about going to Ensenada and how much fun the party scene would be at the contest and in town. After awhile they decided to leave. Bobby was a little shaky on his feet but Ramon looked okay. Ramon's been living at the Peace and Atonement Brotherhood compound out in Sycamore Grove. I didn't think he could just take off without checking with them first. He's in some kind of program there. So I asked him about it before they left, but he shrugged it off."

"He's found religion, huh? Or is it just that's he found someplace to live?"

"I don't know, man. I've tried to talk to him about it before but all he says is that he feels like he's part of something really big. He came by the park last week and he had money to burn. Man, he bought beer for *everyone*."

"Is he working?"

Caesar shook his head and laughed. "The Lord will provide!"

We both laughed and I headed across the parking lot to my truck.

"Take it easy, Caesar," I called over my shoulder.

"Oh, you *know* I will!"

Chapter 2

SOUTH OF THE BORDER

I felt like I'd gathered all the information I could on this side of the border, so it was time to head for Baja. I pulled into my office's parking lot just after Wayne arrived. We got the surfboards out of the storage room and while he packed them into the truck, I went into the gift shop area to tell Claudia that we were headed to Mexico for a few days.

Before we got on the I-5, we made a quick stop at my house for a few more items but it wasn't long before we were heading south. Wayne and I are hardcore Baja travelers. His camper-overcab sleeps two comfortably and has all the amenities plus fourwheel drive, built-up suspension and a bumper winch for those emergency situations. As we set off, we made some cracks about feeling like "Dog the Bounty Hunter." We've taken off for weeks at a time to the beautiful, isolated beaches of Baja Sur, but we've never made the trip to fetch a wayward surfer.

Wayne can be somewhat difficult for the uninitiated to understand but there is nobody more reliable to have around when there is hard work that needs to be done. Wayne has what is commonly referred to as a "short fuse" and doesn't spend a great deal of time contemplating the consequences of his actions. He does spend a lot of time at the gym training in mixed martial arts. Physically, he's no giant — about 6' 2" and 210 pounds — and he looks every bit the devout surfer but once you stand alongside Wayne, you get the sense of his sheer physical strength.

Wayne's father, who raised his son on his own, was a recruiting officer for the Marine Corps. Wayne spent his childhood in a tug of war between the demands of his straight-laced authoritarian father and the beckoning call of the beach. He did his best to honor his father's wishes but there was always an undercurrent of tension and conflict, which resulted in his spending his senior year in a military academy. When I saw him at the beach again some years later, he had served a hitch in the Navy. Wayne never talked about his military service, and if not for the Navy SEAL tattoo on his upper bicep, you'd never know he had served his country.

Wayne has one other tattoo. On the inside of his lower lip is the word "surf." I suppose the stark difference between his tattoos is a reflection of his childhood conflict between duty and freedom. Wayne has long since settled back into civilian life and to most people he appears to be a big blond-headed surfer who works construction and is heavily into martial arts. Pretty straightforward but I sometimes wonder who or what demons he's trying to punish with those ferocious blows he delivers to the heavy bag in the gym.

As we drove, I discussed the situation with Wayne and told him how stressed Paul was about Bobby's strange trip with Ramon amidst the building competition for the world's number-one surfing title. There are only two contests remaining — one at G-land, a left-hand reef break on the east coast of the island of Java, and the most famous contest of all at the Banzai Pipeline in Hawaii.

Each of the major surf clothing and gear companies has a surf team and each sponsors one or more of the 12 contests held annually. Top surfers stand to make millions and their sponsors billions and, as such, competition is fierce and tends to break down along nationalistic lines: US, Australia, Brazil, Japan, South Africa, Tahiti, France, Portugal, Britain, Spain, Ireland, Puerto Rico and, of course, the Hawaiians, who don't like to be lumped in with the mainlanders.

We were going to arrive at San Miguel late so we decided to spend the night at a spot along the coast. First thing in the morning we'd start looking for Bobby. We'd check the contest, then, if need be, go talk with Eduardo and see what he knew about Ramon and Bobby's whereabouts.

With the first phase of our plan set, Wayne launched into the gory details of his latest mixed martial arts sparring match. Long story short: "I annihilated a Jujitsu black belt with a series of strikes to the head."

Occasionally, Wayne succeeds in persuading me to accompany him to the gym and he never tires of explaining, demonstrating and trying to teach me basic martial arts skills. It's not that Wayne is an angry or violent person; he just chooses to live his life on a more primal level than most people. I smiled as he emphasized his story with a punch to the glove compartment. Hanging with him tends to keep a person well-grounded in the here and now.

As we continued south on I-5 towards the border, I started getting that familiar "anything can happen and probably will" feeling that makes Baja travel so enjoyable. I drove through Tijuana with no stops — I treat that city like an old girlfriend: we have some good memories but I don't want to go there again.

We merged onto the coast road, continuing past the surf spots that dot the coastline. After about half an hour, we pulled into a parking area on a bluff overlooking a beach break — the waves were perfect with not a soul in sight.

It is very rare to find good waves that aren't crowded given the number of people who have taken up the sport, but every once in awhile, it is still possible to get lucky. As we walked down the trail to the beach, we saw some incredible waves peel off, but with no one on the waves it can be hard to judge size, shape and other factors. Low-lying clouds were spread across the late afternoon sky and it was very quiet as we began to paddle out. I felt like I was trespassing in a situation not meant for people but reserved for the perfection of nature. However, as soon as we hit the water, Wayne started happily yelling at the top of his lungs and snapped me out of my own quiet thoughts.

We surfed perfect waves until it was too dark to see, then toweled off, got back in the camper and headed down the dirt road to a restaurant we'd found on a previous trip. I'm not sure I should be calling it a restaurant since it's a house in a mobile home community, but the ladies that live there make the best carnitas tacos I've ever had, so it's a first-class eatery in my book. Wayne and I sat at one of the tables on the big covered porch and ate, drank and told stories until it was time to drive back up to the bluff to park and turn in for the night.

* * * * *

In the early morning, a little squall moved through so we woke up to wind, rain and clouds. We had coffee in the camper and continued on our way.

San Miguel is a right-hand break located some five miles north of the city of Ensenada. The waves are fairly well-shaped and consistent but there is one peculiar feature: a rock jetty projects out from the beach by about 100 yards. On most days, the waves flow right into the jetty but on bigger days, it's possible to ride past the tip of the jetty and continue down the beach for a very long ride.

To save us some time, Wayne parked up on the road so we could avoid the hassle of finding a spot in the already-crowded lot. As we walked down the trail to the beach, we could see that the contest hadn't yet started. The waves were bordering on big but they were bumpy.

Surfers and sponsors were making preparations while onlookers were milling about, talking and laughing. Wayne and I almost immediately began encountering familiar faces. We asked everyone the same question. "You seen Bobby Contraras?"

Nobody had seen him. This particular event wasn't as put together as most contests; it was really more like a big party than a surf contest. The nearest thing to a contest official was a guy running around with a megaphone and a clipboard. I grabbed him.

"Bro, I would know if Bobby Contraras was entered in this contest." He assured me, "He's not scheduled to compete."

Wayne and I split up — he took the beach and I handled the parking lot. The whole area was on course for a big fiesta. The surfing community is not generally known for restraint and people were starting early with the rum and Coke and other assorted party favors. After an hour of searching with no results it became clear that our missing surfer was a no-show at San Miguel.

Wayne and I headed into town to continue our search. Downtown Ensenada was packed with visitors all looking for a good time and at midday Hussongs Cantina was standing room only. Two guys were working the door, which looked like it meant helping carry people out of the bar to be transported to jail. I took a guess and picked the smaller of the two doormen.

"Eduardo?"

He raised his eyebrows, which I took as a yes. I stuck out my hand for a handshake. "Crazy Caesar from

Encinitas is a friend of mine. He said I should stop by and say hello. I'm Mike and this is Wayne. Caesar thought you might be able to help us out."

Eduardo focused his attention on a couple of giggling girls and their IDs. He waved them in.

"Caesar said your English is good but that you might not want to talk. We just need a little help."

Eduardo sat down on a bar stool that was next to the door and smiled. "Crazy Caesar's not so crazy, right? I don't think that guy's worked since before I was born! I'm the crazy one working at this madhouse. So, what's up?"

"We're looking for Ramon. He's with a friend of ours, Bobby Contraras, and Bobby's needed back in the States right away, it's kind of a family emergency. He's not answering his phone and his sister is freaking out. I guess Ramon doesn't have a phone so we haven't been able to get a hold of either of them. Ramon said he was going to be visiting family here and Caesar said you could give us directions to the house."

"I don't see a problem since Caesar sent you guys to see me. Ramon came by here last night on his way to his mom's house. He borrowed my key to their gate."

He laughed. "Yeah, he actually paid me back some money he owed me. Usually he's trying to borrow money, not pay it back!"

Wayne spoke up. "Was Bobby with him?"

"Nah, he was by himself. He didn't stay long. You know, I told him it was the first time I've ever seen him turn down a free beer. Yeah, he was in a hurry; he just wanted my key. Who knows what happened to his, but he better bring mine back."

He leaned inside the doorway and whistled to get the bartender's attention and then gave him the thumbs up.

"Go inside and grab a beer. If you bring me something to write on, I'll draw you guys a map to the house. What kind of car are you driving?"

"Four-wheel drive truck." Wayne answered.

"Good." He laughed again. "You're going to need it."

* * * * *

Following Eduardo's map drawn on a paper place mat, we headed out of town east towards the foothills. We quickly became lost, but no surprise there. Although my Spanish is pretty bad, I can generally make myself understood so I started asking for directions. Eduardo told us the family had an old, large restaurant sign in the shape of a rooster in the front yard. Eduardo explained about the sign.

"The family got the sign from a restaurant that went out of business and they liked it so much they decided to put it in their front yard."

As we got closer to the house, directions became easier. I'd ask "¿Donde esta la casa con el signo del gallo?" which means, "Where's the house with the rooster sign?"

When going off-road, no matter how good your vehicle may be, it's always advisable to proceed with caution. As we made our way towards the house, what had been passing for a road became more like a sandy wash so I got out and walked ahead and directed Wayne. Eventually we passed through an open gate located at the top of a small hill. In the valley below, the rooster sign was hard to miss — it was nearly as tall as the house.

Wayne pulled up. "What are they, cock fighters?" he called out the window.

I got in the truck. As soon as we reached the house a pack of small noisy dogs swarmed the vehicle, closely followed by several young kids. Greetings were exchanged and I asked if they'd seen Ramon and Bobby.

"¿Donde estan Ramon y Bobby?"

The oldest child pointed down the road. "Estan en la casa de montana."

We were being directed to a "mountain house" on the other side of the valley.

"Gracias."

We continued on for about a mile before the road started winding uphill. About halfway up the mountain, we saw Bobby's dusty Subaru station wagon parked alongside the wash, near a path that traversed the face of the steep boulder-strewn hillside. We parked and got out and Wayne yelled for Bobby. I leaned in and honked the horn and Wayne called his name again. No response so we locked up the camper and started up the path. Near the top, we began to see signs of an encampment and at the top we saw an open covered lean-to. I walked towards it.

"Bobby? Hey, it's Mike. Ramon!"

I poked my head inside the lean-to and came face-to-face with what used to be Ramon, sitting against a large boulder. Lifeless eyes stared back at me from a swollen and bruised face. He'd been strangled; the garrote left around his neck.

I let out a "Whoa!" and was ready for a very speedy exit from that part of the world but Wayne had other ideas. He pushed past me and immediately began searching Ramon's pockets.

"Wayne, while you're doing that I'm going to keep looking around. I'd like to get out of here as soon as we can. I sure hope I don't find Bobby in the same condition as Ramon." I reluctantly started to check around the camp. The "mountain house," as the kids had called it, was an abandoned sort of survivalist camp with a multimillion-dollar view from the blue Pacific on one side of the

27

mountaintop to the vast desert to the east. The camp included a handful of lean-to shelters and cisterns carved out of the rock for storing rainwater. I could see by the footprints in the sandy soil that people had been in the area and a fire pit had recently been in use.

There were also several rock shelters with fire-blackened overhangs. These were probably Indian and quite old. I ventured into one and nearly stumbled over Bobby. I quickly checked to make sure he was breathing — he was alive but unconscious. He had a leg wound that was bound with bloody rags. I wondered if Bobby's attackers were still in the area.

The situation was now actively life-threatening. Being on the wrong side of the border with a dead body and a badly injured world-class surfer is not my idea of fun. At times like these, it's hard to control the instinct for self-preservation. In other words, "Run for your life!"

"Wayne, over here. I found Bobby!" I yelled at the top of my lungs.

I was still trying to figure out what to do as Wayne ducked around me, squatted down next to Bobby and started taking his pulse. "Slow and regular."

He checked Bobby's leg. "He doesn't seem to be bleeding. The dressing on his wound should hold him for awhile. His eyes are fixed and dilated, his skin is cold and he's in shock. We have to get this kid to a hospital."

All that information inside of 10 seconds; Wayne's military training was coming into play.

"Yes, hospital. Right, right, right." I needed some time to think as I wandered around with my cell phone up in the air trying to get a signal. "No reception so we need to get him down off this mountain. Looks like the surfboard-and-duct-tape routine is our only option. Hustle down to the truck."

Wayne started jogging toward the path. "Same as that guy who fell off the cliff in Cabo that time — yep, that'll work. Be right back."

Bobby was not responding to my voice or gentle shaking. I had no idea whether his unconscious state was due to injury or drugs, but I did know that he should be immobilized. Was duct taping Bobby to Wayne's surfboard the best course of action? Maybe not, but Bobby needed to be securely transported and it's all we had. Thankfully, Bobby's a small wiry kid so we were able to get him down the hill and into the truck without too much difficulty.

Wayne started up the truck and we proceeded slowly and carefully back up the wash, with me in back to watch Bobby.

"Listen Wayne, I'm still not getting a cell signal and even if I could, by the time we get a Life Flight helicopter rescue worked out with all the red tape involved it would probably be faster just to drive to the border."

Wayne turned and looked back at me through the cab opening. "I hear what you're saying. It's probably best just to get him back to the States where Paul can get him the best care money can buy. Plus, we won't get asked a bunch of questions that we can't answer anyway because we don't know what happened."

"Bottom line is if somebody comes across Ramon's body you, me, and Bobby could be down here trying to explain ourselves for a very long time. If that happens you know the authorities aren't going to let Bobby leave to get medical attention."

Wayne said, "It's decided then. We head back to San Diego as quickly and carefully as possible. Just keep a real close watch on his breathing and make sure that leg wound doesn't start bleeding."

The drive back from Ensenada takes about six hours. Cell phone service proved to be spotty but eventually I was able to get through to Paul, who was relieved we had Bobby but couldn't believe Ramon was dead.

"Let me make sure I understand what you're saying, Ramon is dead? As in not breathing?"

"Not just dead. Murdered. Strangled. That's right Paul, he's gone and we don't know why or who did it. But one thing's for sure; we're not going to hang around and ask questions. For now, all we want to do is get back on our side of the border. Can you get an ambulance and meet us at the Denny's Restaurant parking lot near the San Ysidro border crossing? We should be there in about two hours."

Paul was starting to get over his initial shock. "I'll be there with an ambulance and doctor. Just get here as fast as you can! No, forget that! Drive slowly and be careful. It's probably best not to move him any more than absolutely necessary."

Bobby remained unconscious the entire trip.

Chapter 3

BACK IN THE U.S.A

You can say what you want about the U.S. but if you're arrested for a crime here you do have rights. Mexico? I'm not so sure. So Wayne and I were greatly relieved when we crossed the border with no hassle. We met Paul and the ambulance in the parking lot as planned. Bobby, still duct taped to Wayne's board, was whisked away to the hospital.

Wayne and I had succeeded in bringing Bobby back but we now had many more questions than answers on our hands. The whole situation made no sense. What was the motive? No wallets or cash had been taken and Bobby's car had been abandoned.

It was late when Wayne dropped me at my house. As I walked through my front door, I gave my customary yell, "Honey I'm home!" I knew that, as usual, the house would be empty but for some reason, it makes me feel good to say it.

My wife of 18 years, Cathy, left me for a local bartender and then left him too and blamed the whole thing on "the change of life." The change of life thing is probably true, but I've never really been able to forgive and forget so now we live separate lives. However, we still share many financial assets as well as an adult daughter so we're in frequent contact. This arrangement has been going on for almost two years with no end or legal divorce in sight.

I got into bed and went right to sleep. Both my brain and my body were used up from stress and tension.

* * * * *

As soon as I woke up, I called the hospital but the staff wouldn't give me details on Bobby's condition. Paul wasn't answering his cell phone so I left a message.

I picked up around the house a bit while I waited for the coffee to brew. I live in a Cape Cod colonial style built around 1954; I bought it from the original owners. Over the years, I've built and lived in houses all over Encinitas, but I always seem to return to this one. It's small but comfortable and one of the main attractions is its proximity to the beach.

I've found that as I've gotten older, I have more time to surf and I enjoy surfing more than I did in my younger years. At this stage in life, my days are primarily focused on surfing. Everything else is arranged around wind, tides and swell direction. Sometimes I feel like a surfer who took 20 years off to accumulate possessions, earn a living, put some money in the bank and raise a family. Naturally, there are times when I have an obligation that can't be avoided but I keep those situations to a minimum. Some days, when I'm waiting for the best time to go surfing, it's necessary to check the surf four or five times so being close to the beach is very important — it cuts down on the worry over missing good waves, which can destroy any chance of concentrating on work or other jobs.

My phone rang. It was Paul.

"I've been at the hospital most of the night with Maria. Bobby is stable. Those bastards cut the Achilles tendon in his right leg so he has to have reconstructive surgery this morning."

"Does he remember what happened?"

"Well, he's pretty drugged up right now but he said he doesn't remember being attacked. He recalls having a few beers with Ramon and some other guys around the campfire Wednesday night, but after that things are very vague. The doctor says that his memory may come back after he has time to rest and recover."

"Man that's a lot of time to lose track of. He must have been out of it."

"Yeah, I know. Listen, Mike, I've gotta finish up the paperwork for his operation. Thanks again for bringing him home. Why don't we meet up at my house around noon and we can talk about what to do next."

"Sounds good. Give Maria my best and tell her I'll be by."

I heard the coffeemaker beep. Time to grab a cup and head for surf check numero uno.

* * * * *

A few minutes later, I was standing at the bluff-top viewpoint, along with some of the other regulars, deciding that there would be no early morning surf session. Most of the guys were trying to get in a quick surf before going to work or taking the kids to school. Contrary to popular belief, they don't have ridiculously stupid nicknames or end every sentence with "dude." But that's not to say that there isn't the usual assortment of oddballs and characters among the group.

Marty is always good for a laugh. He never accepts any type of "normal" job, instead he's always working on a new "get rich quick" scheme of some type. So far there's been gold and uranium mining, hot air balloon rides, candle-making, beach metal detection and computer recycling. Those are just the ones I can remember; the list goes on. His latest venture is Christmas tree light installation. When the guys started poking fun at him, I thought his comeback was pretty good. "Yes, the work is seasonal. But don't forget, after I install the lights, they'll need me to go back and take them all down."

Then there's Daryl who's a stay-at-home dad. He arrives at the beach most mornings pushing a stroller containing his 18-month-old son. Daryl's standard line is: "I don't have time to work. I already have a full-time job arguing with my wife."

Daryl used to own a sheet metal shop but is now, as he puts it "RR'd," short for Recession Retired. The current economy is putting a lot of stress and strain on many marriages, with the divorce attorneys reaping the benefits.

Soon, I was the only one staring at the water. I thought about Bobby and about this small town where he'd grown up. Encinitas is really nothing special; it began as an agricultural community in the early 19th century and during the 1940s and 1950s was a stopover destination for people traveling from Los Angeles to San Diego and Mexico. When the nearby racetrack opened with the slogan "Where the Turf Meets the Surf," North County, as this region of San Diego County is called, found a place on the map and during the 1960s, the area started growing rapidly and hasn't stopped since.

Encinitas, which became a city in 1986, is made up of five communities: Leucadia, Cardiff-by-the-Sea, New Encinitas, Olivenhain, and Old Encinitas. While Encinitas used to be known as the flower capital of the world, southern California is a pressure cooker of development and time ran out on agriculture's economic viability in the city.

Of all the communities, Leucadia stands out for its laid-back vibe and funky commercial corridor along Highway 101. It is, along with all the other areas, to some extent a bedroom community to San Diego and Los Angeles and is home to a large number of homegrown artists and retired hippies.

Cardiff has a different feel. State beaches and campgrounds cover Cardiff's stretch of coastline so the ocean is visible from all of downtown and the view is part of the everyday patterns of life. The community's hillside layout and limited coastal development allow Cardiff to gaze out at the ocean, while Leucadia looks at itself. "Cardiffians" live in a true southern California beach community. And they pay for the privilege — homes with prominent ocean views sell for upwards of a million dollars.

New Encinitas, located inland along the famous El Camino Real, came into existence as a result of the urban sprawl of the 1970s. This area is kind of like the acknowledged, yet not quite accepted, stepchild of Old Encinitas — everybody knows its there but nobody wants to talk about it. New Encinitas is also home to the fierce and predatory species known as the "soccer mom."

Olivenhain is what passes for our rural area. Located about five miles inland, residents enjoy two-acre zoning and there's a mix of agriculture and horse properties. Just east of Olivenhain is Rancho Santa Fe, one of the highest per capita income areas in the country so some people facetiously refer to Olivenhain as the "poor man's Rancho Santa Fe." The community was meant to provide all the amenities of a rural lifestyle while still being close to the ocean. Unfortunately, its narrow roads can't support modern traffic volume. Olivenhain lies between two population centers, which means commuter traffic jams the roads, making it a great place to live if you don't have to go anywhere.

Old Encinitas was built up around Highway 101 and is in many ways a hybrid of Leucadia and Cardiff but it's less beachy than Cardiff and more developed than Leucadia. Old Encinitas is also the seat of our local government. I say "seat" because sometimes it's difficult to tell the difference between that part of our anatomy and our local councilpersons and their decisions. Five council members are elected to make wise decisions on our behalf. Currently, the council is comprised of two women, who are mostly liberal, and three men who are mostly conservative. The men always vote against the women. I call it the rule of the "gang of three." At the present time, the "gang of three" is in the process of placing a totally inappropriate sports park, complete with multiple 90-foot light poles, in the middle of the peaceful little community of Cardiff. Only time will tell what will happen with this political hot potato but one thing's for sure: small town government is never dull.

Somehow, Old Encinitas has managed to preserve the quality of a slower-paced lifestyle, perhaps because the land was originally subdivided into reasonably large lots, which prevented the usual coastal congestion. Also, the existence of historic scenic Highway 101, which carries the coastal traffic through town, helped save the area from dense development.

The ocean and the beauty of its coastline attract all types of people to Encinitas. Numerous religious groups have settled in the area, giving the city a distinct spiritual essence. You have your typical denominations such as Catholic, Presbyterian, Jewish and Baptist but there are also Eastern Religions such as Hinduism and Buddhism and numerous splinter groups. One of those groups, the Peace and Atonement Brotherhood, is very popular with the local residents. I don't know much about what the PAB, as it's known, represents but from what I've gathered over the years, its goal is something like "total self-enlightenment through meditation and selfless devotion to our principles."

Sounds like a tall order to me.

I'd still say surfing is the biggest religion around these parts. Encinitas is also a center of the huge skateboarding industry. And while these industries are cranking, it's still possible, on occasion, to have some waves to yourself — when there's any to have, that is.

I'd kept my eye out for Caesar at the beach this morning; I felt it was my responsibility to tell him about Ramon. It certainly wasn't ideal that Wayne and I had left Ramon where we found him, but let's face it, he didn't mind at this point and he was protected from the elements. I didn't know if Ramon was a good guy but I didn't get the impression that he was a real bad guy. Either way, we needed to know what happened. I wondered if there would be a service for him at the PAB compound, since he had been living there before he died.

I went over to my office. It was Sunday so the bus depot was deserted and the gift shop hadn't opened yet. In a few minutes, the local dive bar would be starting its Sunday football brunch buffet — laid out on one of the pool tables — so I walked over to check for Caesar there.

The Daley Double Saloon has the typical double swinging doors, a long mahogany bar down one side of the main room, booths down the other side and pool tables and eating area at the far end. The saloon has been in the same location for the last 60 years. The bar is basically a throwback to the time when Encinitas was mostly a rural farm and ranch community. Nowadays, it's very popular with the trendy crowd but it retains its grass roots clientele.

One of the numerous stories associated with the bar is about a brawl that occurred in the mid-1980s. Supposedly, a group of government Secret Service agents, in town as part of a detail to guard the vice president, got in a dispute with a group of locals. The dispute ended up in a fight that traveled up and down Highway 101 until it was broken up by the Sheriff's department. One of the agents was rumored to have bitten off a portion of his opponent's ear. The whole affair was kept quiet by the government. True? Who knows, but it makes for a good story.

I pulled up a stool and the bartender, Jerry, cracked an Anchor Steam for me. It's safe to say I'm a beer snob and I've put a lot of work into it. After a very thorough, logical and exhaustive search for the best domestic beer, I've decided Anchor Steam gets the blue ribbon. Of course, this excludes porters and stouts, which fall into different categories. My buddy from the beach, Dwayne, sat down next to me.

"Hear about Clyde Arrington?"

I took a big swig of beer and grunted a "Hello" and a "No" at the same time.

"He's dead," Dwayne said. "Died at Mavericks this morning. Get this, he was found floating face down and was pulled out by some guy on a jet ski. Maybe a heart attack or something, who knows — crazy, right?"

I asked Jerry to turn the TV to ESPN. They were recapping the sports news of the day. Arrington was a top-10 surfer. Could there be a connection between what happened to Bobby and Arrington's sudden death? Was it a coincidence that now another contender was out of the competition?

I told myself to get a grip. My imagination was running a little wild.

Mavericks flashed on the screen, first the lineup and then a crowd in the parking lot gathered near an ambulance. Some people had their arms around each other. A woman was crying. On the edge of the crowd, several people stood together, dressed similarly in white shirts, ties and black pants — the Peace and Atonement Brotherhood uniform. One guy among the group was wearing a full robe.

I drained most of my beer.

Dwayne shook his head and turned to me again. "Crazy, right?"

Crazy. Right.

My cell phone rang as I walked out of the bar. It was Paul.

"Have you heard the news about Arrington at Mavericks?"

"Yeah, I just heard. That makes two top-10 surfers out of the competition in two days."

"Something is wrong, stuff like this just doesn't happen," Paul said. "I'm sure the police and probably the Coast Guard will investigate but it sure seems suspicious to me."

"I agree. Listen, I'm still trying to track down Caesar to give him the bad news about Ramon. See you at your place in a while."

Caesar had taken his show on the road. This time I found him in Cardiff hanging around Glen Park, a beautiful little grassy park across Highway 101 from the state campground and the ocean. Caesar was surprisingly calm about Ramon's death. Maybe living on the streets gives you a different perspective about the permanence of human life. He said he would notify the rest of the family on both sides of the border.

"Did anybody have it out for Ramon, Caesar?"

"Nah, the kid was harmless. His biggest problem was he could never really make up his mind about what he wanted to do in life, he kind of just drifted from one thing to another. That's probably why he liked the PAB so much — all the decisions were made for him and all he had to do was go along with the program."

* * * * *

I arrived at Paul's house around noon as arranged. In the driveway, a few guys were pushing around on their skateboards, practicing tricks.

I rang the front doorbell and Paul answered before the bell stopped ringing. I followed him upstairs to the living room, which is oriented towards an all-glass wall. I admired the forever views toward the ocean and the overall design concept of the house, a box within a box overlooking the valley below, with many loft areas, decks, pipe railing and glazing. Along the side of the living room, the top half of the indoor waterfall was visible. Water gently flowed down the face to the reflecting pool on the first floor.

White Sand Surf team manager Ellie McPherson was seated on the couch surrounded by papers and magazines. I know Ellie from the beach. She's a 30-something blue-eyed blonde who looks good in a two-piece at the beach but I'd never really been able to get too close; there were always too many guys following her around. Ellie had been a fairly well-known competitive surfer before she retired.

Paul sat down in an armchair and motioned for me to do the same. "Mike, you know that as team manager, Ellie is aware of everything that has happened and will be kept in the loop on everything from here on out."

I nodded in Ellie's direction and she briefly smiled at me before returning her attention to Paul, whose voice sounded strained. He was probably ready to melt down with stress, worry and lack of sleep. Bobby's recovery and road back would be painful and slow and consequently, his life as a competitive surfer might be over. That potential reality could severely threaten Paul's chances of taking his company multinational.

"I intend to find out who attacked Bobby and why it happened. So far all we know is that he went to Mexico with Ramon. We have to find out why. Any thoughts, Mike?"

"Well, I'm hoping that once Bobby has a chance to recover he'll be able to give us something to go on. Until then, we can only focus on Ramon. I suppose I can check around and see what I can turn up on him."

Paul's knee was bouncing up and down as he talked. "Now, we have Arrington dead at Mavericks this morning. That's two top-10 rated surfers out of the competition in less than a week. I don't believe in coincidences."

Paul walked over to an intercom on the wall and called Josh Phillips, who was outside skating, to come upstairs. Josh is on the surf team. He's not a superstar like Bobby, but he definitely has potential and is currently ranked in the top 10. Turns out Josh had been up at Mavericks this morning.

"Josh, tell Mike."

"Well, I got to the parking area before it got light and was waiting around with a bunch of other guys for the tide and wind to get better so we could paddle out. Arrington was there with the rest of us."

"Anything unusual or out of ordinary that you can remember?"

"No, not really, just that there were definitely more PAB members around than I'd ever seen before. They were all handing out pamphlets and doing their conversion routine. Arrington was pissed because he had to chase a bunch of the PAB guys away from his truck. He thought they were trying to steal stuff out of the back. But, no, man, it was just a typical surf day — until they found Arrington floating face down."

Ellie said she wanted to go over travel details with Josh so he followed her into one of the offices. Josh and the rest of the surf team were heading to Indonesia in a few days for the next leg of the Pro Tour.

Paul started pacing along behind the couch. He said he planned on going to the police but didn't expect them to do much about a crime that happened in Mexico — cooperation between the U.S. and Mexico on a local case of this type would be almost non-existent. "Until Bobby gets better all we have is Ramon. I want to know what was going on between him and Bobby. Were they really friends? What did they have in common? Was Ramon trying to convert Bobby to PAB? If he was trying to convert Bobby, he was certainly going about it in a strange way."

He stopped pacing and looked at me. "I know this is costing you money by taking up your time, Mike, so keep track of it and I'll pay you your hourly rate. Is that okay?"

"Save your money for now, Paul. I'll check around and see what I can find out."

From Paul's house, I went home and then jumped on my bike for a quick ride down to the beach. On the way, I remembered that one of my old acquaintances from the beach, John Hayward, was involved with the PAB. Maybe he could be a source of information on Ramon.

John had moved from Encinitas to Hawaii several years back. He settled in a remote area of one of the outer islands, took up a daily routine of drugs and surfing and went off the deep end. Eventually, his mental health deteriorated to the point that he was sent back to the mainland to live with his relatives. He entered treatment when he returned to Encinitas and was diagnosed as schizophrenic. Whether or not John's condition was genetic, his excessive drug use certainly damaged his mental health.

For a long time after John came back from the islands, I saw him at the beach and he wouldn't say a word to me. But gradually, with his treatment and medication, he became more talkative and it was now possible to hold a conversation with him. His involvement with the Brotherhood seemed to be part of his recovery.

The waves looked fun so I grabbed my board for an afternoon session. A surfer is similar to a sailor in many ways, always aware of the surf, weather conditions, and tides. The local beach break is usually best — depending on the swell — about one hour after low tide. Less water means faster waves and the incoming tide helps add a little size. If you don't mind walking down the beach, it's also possible to get some uncrowded waves.

To put it in the simplest terms, surfing is fun. I once had a conversation with a racecar driver and the subject of surfing came up. He asked me, "Do you remember what happens on a wave after you've finished your ride?"

I'd never really thought about it before, but I answered honestly. "I only remember certain things that happen on the wave. Everything happens so quickly it's kind of a blur and you're relying on your conditioning, training and instinct."

"That's what I thought," he replied. "It's the same with racing. You start down the track and before you know it, it's over. You don't think about it, you just do it."

Time does seem to stand still on a wave and when your ride's over, all you're left with is a feeling. If you were able to do all the various maneuvers you attempted on the wave it's a good feeling. If your attempted maneuvers failed it's a bad feeling - plus you end up under water. Surfing is the ultimate escape because all other thoughts, distractions and irritations of everyday life fade away and you're completely living in the moment.

The November conditions — clear blue sky, white sand, 70-degree weather, and moderate swell — taken all together acted as a tonic for my soul. I surfed until dark, which is always a good way to end another day in paradise. When I finally came in, I felt ready to start the next phase of what had become my investigation.

* * * * *

Back at home, there was a message from Cathy waiting for me on the answering machine. I sighed and decided to return her call tomorrow. I also concluded, after a look in the fridge, that since there was nothing worth eating, I'd go downtown for dinner. Since my separation, I've established a well-worn path that winds through downtown from one restaurant or bar to the next. There's an art to going out to eat alone. I've found that if I take a book or newspaper with me and appear to be intently reading people will, reluctantly, leave me be. The trick is to never stay at one place long enough to wear out your welcome.

Chapter 4

OPEN SERVICE

During my surf check Monday morning, I "happened" to run into John Hayward and as we chatted, I gradually brought the subject around to the Brotherhood.

John is tall and lanky with shoulder-length brown hair and a scraggly beard, so he looks the part of a partially flipped-out religious zealot but when he's on meds, he's very calm and has a slow and deliberate manner of speaking. He has one of those all-terrain faces full of sun-induced lines and cracks. When he was 25 years old, he looked like he was approaching middle age. He's looked the same ever since so now it's working in his favor. Unlike other PAB members, he's always dressed casually, like any other surfer hanging at the beach, in a T-shirt, jeans and sneakers.

Lucky for me, John was more than willing to talk even if at first it sounded like he was reading from a script. "The goal of the Peace and Atonement Brotherhood is total self-enlightenment through meditation and selfless devotion to certain principles laid down by the founder. There are many levels of enlightenment, from initiate to master."

"Sounds pretty cool, John. Hey, did you hear that Wayne and I found Bobby Contraras down in Ensenada on Saturday? He was badly hurt and we had to bring him back and take him to the hospital."

"Yeah, I heard. A bunch of guys down here were talking about it yesterday. That must have been pretty hairy bringing him back like that. How's he doing?"

"He's having surgery on his leg and we're all hoping for the best. He doesn't remember very much about what happened except that he went down to Mex with Ramon. You know Ramon?"

"Yeah, Ramon. Too bad, man. Was it some kind of accident? Driving down there can be really dangerous."

I decided to avoid going into details about Ramon's death. Telling John the truth would just complicate the situation. "Don't know. The authorities down there are looking into the situation. Wayne and I just grabbed Bobby and left. What can you tell me about Ramon? He joined PAB, right?"

"I really didn't know him very well, I only talked to him a couple of times. He was living at the Sycamore Grove compound, which is ordinarily reserved for monks who are serious students of the true path and Ramon was only a new member, so that was unusual. And I know he was spending a lot of time with a group of visiting monks from the Santa Cruz compound who are much more advanced — way above his level."

"Any particular reason Ramon seemed to be getting this special treatment?"

John shrugged his shoulders. "That I really couldn't tell you. I just kind of assumed that one of the higher ups had taken a special interest in him for some reason. You know if you're interested in the Brotherhood, you're more than welcome to attend tonight's open service. It's out at the Sycamore Grove compound at six o'clock."

I accepted John's invitation. I'd never been to a PAB service and I was more than a little curious. Besides, what could it hurt?

The swell was building rapidly, filling in from the north, so I decided to try another one of my favorite breaks where it's possible to get some waves to myself. I was able to get in a good session with several of my surf bros before the swell increased and the waves got too big and began to close out.

* * * * *

When I got home, I had some time before the evening service at the temple so I sat down at the computer to do some background reading on the Brotherhood. The few details I already knew about the organization had mainly to do with its local real estate holdings. Over the years, I've done a couple of building projects for the Brotherhood and in the process I've gotten to know Harvey Patel, who handles business development for the organization. I'm leery of organized religious groups and never felt more than just a mild curiosity about the Brotherhood's teachings. My relationship with Harvey has always been friendly, but strictly professional, and he's never tried to convert or indoctrinate me to his beliefs.

The Brotherhood is probably the biggest landowner in Encinitas; it acquired prime land when it was still cheap and has received other properties over the years through member bequests. As a religious group, the Brotherhood pays no taxes and from what I've seen, the organization is treated with a great deal of respect by the city fathers, which is understandable because of its reputation of caring about the local community. That said, I think the Brotherhood's image is also bolstered by the fact that its temples and shrines attract visitors from around the world who bring the all-mighty tourist dollars to Encinitas.

From my online research, I learned that the Brotherhood was established in the early 1940s in California before going global and is divided into secular and spiritual branches. While its ultimate spiritual leader is headquartered in India, there are also local spiritual

47

leaders. Patel, it turns out, is a bigger cheese than I realized — he heads the local secular side of the Brotherhood.

The compound where I was to meet John for the service is in Sycamore Grove, a rural community about 15 miles inland from Encinitas. While the location seems naturally private enough — off the main highway and at the end of a narrow road that winds along the coastal foothills — the roughly 10-acre property is surrounded on all sides by an ominous eight-foot block wall.

I pulled into the parking lot shortly before 5:00 p.m. so I had plenty of time to stroll around before the 6:00 p.m. service. In the compound are several large dormitory type buildings, a meeting hall, what appear to be the head offices and assorted out buildings. Large oak trees around the property give the grounds a rather gloomy appearance but the gardens and meditation areas, which are open daily to the public, are first-rate.

Most of the people I saw were dressed casually with the exception of what I knew to be Brotherhood initiates, who wore shirts, slacks and ties. The rookies are expected to go into the neighborhoods each day and spread the word. There were also several monks who wore the long full robe complete with hood so that their faces were barely visible. I passed by one monk walking in the opposite direction. We made eye contact and I was surprised to recognize Frank James, an Encinitas City Council member. In all the years I've followed city government I had no idea that Councilman James was a member of the Brotherhood. While I was wandering, I also saw Harvey Patel. He was hurrying across the courtyard and we gave each other a quick wave hello.

John Hayward and I met in the courtyard area and he suggested that we head to the meeting hall where the service would be held. I remembered to ask him if he could point out the monks who had been hanging around with

Ramon. Inside, the meeting hall resembled a large church. The interior was dark wood; candles provided the only lighting and an aisle led to a stage with pew-type bench seating along the sides. There were not very many people in the auditorium and most took seats towards the front. It was a surprisingly ordinary group of people, young and old. John and I settled into seats toward the rear.

The program began with a single robed monk at the podium who delivered a homily on the benefits of good deeds. This was followed by a breathing and meditation period that lasted about 10 minutes. Then came several testimonials by people who espoused the blessings of enlightenment and the true path of the Peace and Atonement Brotherhood.

Just as I started to be lulled by one particularly in-depth testimonial, the entire room was filled with chanting as several monks began walking down each side of the center aisle. Each monk held an incense burner shaped like an upside-down bell and it was just my luck that the last monk in line on my side of the aisle parked the burning incense next to my seat. I looked over at John and he raised his eyebrows and nodded towards the monk who was standing beside me. I assumed he was pointing out one of the monks who had been associating with Ramon. I glanced sideways at the monk and got a fairly good look at his face under the hood. I filed the image away.

Between the pungent fumes of the incense and the chanting, I began to feel kind of out of sorts. A couple of minutes later, as the incense procession began to exit, I started feeling very heavy, and not in a relaxed way. Could I be falling into some sort of a trance? The exit doors opened up. I knew the ceremony was over but I didn't move. I couldn't. John passed by me and I wanted to follow. My mind was telling my body to get up but my legs weren't responding. I felt like I was part of the bench.

I threw my will into overdrive. By the time I finally managed to get up and make my way to the door, the hall was nearly empty. As I stumbled along the garden path towards the parking area, I thought I saw hooded figures following along in the shadows and I was filled with a panic I could not control. I had to get to my truck and get home to safety. I knew I shouldn't be driving in my altered condition but I had to get out of there.

I felt completely disoriented but somehow I managed to pull out of the lot and keep the car in the right lane. My night vision was shot and I began seeing all types of strange apparitions. My arms felt like rubber, my reflexes were wrecked and gauging my speed became more difficult as I continued down the narrow, winding country road. I might have been okay if I hadn't looked in the rear view mirror. There was a vehicle right on my tail and its high beams caused my eyes to dilate, destroying what was left of my already shaky night vision. The last thing I remember clearly was heading into a turn at what I thought was a moderate speed. As I continued along, it became increasingly difficult to remain in my lane. My front right wheel hit the soft shoulder and my truck went flying off into the night.

When I regained consciousness, I was hanging upside-down by my seat belt. I kicked out the shattered windshield, crawled out, and then I just sat there with my head in my hands. I couldn't remember the actual impact but I didn't seem to be hurt, other than a slightly dented forehead. A car pulled over and a couple made their way over to me. I still felt extremely disoriented and didn't even attempt to stand up. I heard someone mention 911 and in what seemed like just a second later, an EMT was checking me out. Time seemed to have wrapped back on itself and the flashing lights and other assorted noises were giving me another round of sensory overload.

The EMT released me and I found myself in the backseat of a Sheriff's car. My incoherent answers to everyone's questions regarding the crash and my condition had earned me a night in the drunk tank.

Monday night wasn't a busy one at the Vista County Jail. Just a few minutes after a male nurse drew some blood to be used against me on a drunk driving charge, I found myself in a holding cell. The whole experience still seemed surreal, although the ache in my head was very real. I spent the night stretched out on a bench against the rear wall of the cell, trying to sleep. Around 9:00 a.m., I was released on my own recognizance. I knew I was being charged with driving under the influence but I was just glad to be out of there.

I got in a cab and, on the way home, began to try to figure out what happened. There was no doubt in my mind that I had some type of a drug hangover; I was sluggish and was having visual and sensory flashbacks. The only thing I really felt capable of doing was sleeping, so when I got home I grabbed a pillow and hit the couch.

I woke up about 1:00 p.m. and opened the blinds. The sun was out. It was a nice Southern California day and it was time to assess the situation. First, I called Bruce, a lawyer I knew who had worked with me on several real estate deals. I liked Bruce because he'd always been efficient, normal and he answered his own phone.

"Hi, Bruce?" I decided to try to make light of the situation. "This is Mike Malone calling fresh out of Vista County Jail."

"Let's hear it. What happened?"

"Well, it all started when I decided to go to a church service."

"Okay?"

"Right now I don't really know how it happened but I can tell you what happened."

I told Bruce what I knew — that I had not been drinking — and what I thought — that somehow I had been drugged. I knew the drugged part was pretty hard to explain because I had not eaten, drank or smoked anything.

"Criminal law is not really my thing," Bruce said. "But I can make a few calls and see what I can find out. You've certainly got an interesting story going here."

"Thanks Bruce, I appreciate your help."

After I hung up the phone, I sat back, closed my eyes and visualized the service. Nothing helpful was coming back. Maybe getting out of my grungy clothes and a hot shower would help to clear my mind. As I walked into the bathroom, I pulled my sweatshirt up over my head and that's when I inhaled a distinct odor — the smell of the incense from the Brotherhood service. That monk had held the pungent incense practically right under my nose. I stood under the shower and let the hot water run down my back. Then it came to me. There must have been something powerful mixed in with that incense because I grew up at the beach and, for better or worse, I know every type of drug out there and I've never been knocked off my feet like that before.

I called Bruce back and told him my incense theory. I knew it didn't make much sense, but it was the only explanation. Whether or not he believed me, he sounded like he did.

Wayne had left a message while I was in the shower. He was checking in to see if I had work for him. I called him back and his solution to my overnight adventure was what I expected.

"We need to go out to the Brotherhood compound and cause the monk with the incense some serious bodily injury."

My mind was still not functioning all that well so I told Wayne to calm down until I could muster some type of game plan.

"Okay, I'm chill," he said. "But keep me posted."

Wayne's direct approach to problems works really well at times and I started to think maybe this was one of those times. My appearance at the PAB service had rattled someone's cage, but why? I had only gone with John out of curiosity and on the outside chance that I might be able to gather some additional information on Ramon. Someone at the compound had overreacted and by doing so had tipped his hand that he had something to hide. Now I was very, very curious. And mad.

Next, I called Paul Maguire.

"I just got back from the hospital, my new second home. Bobby's surgery yesterday went really well. I got him the same doctor who works on all the big professional sport stars and he's optimistic about Bobby's recovery."

"Did you get a chance to ask Bobby any questions about who attacked him? And what about Ramon?"

"Well, first of all, he's still sedated and groggy, but no, so far he still doesn't remember anything about the actual attack. He says Ramon is just a friend of a friend from the beach and they just started talking while they were having some beers and it seemed like a good idea at the time to take a little surf trip and visit Ramon's family in Ensenada. Bobby says Ramon was just down to party and he doesn't remember him saying anything about the PAB. I haven't told him yet that Ramon is dead."

I told Paul about what had happened to me the previous night at the PAB compound with all its weird little twists and turns. When I finished, I had to ask if he was still on the line.

"Yeah, I'm still here. That's one hell of a story. Drugged by incense? That's gotta be a first. Are you all right? I really don't need anymore friends in the hospital right now."

"Yeah, I'm okay, just a dent in my forehead and a totaled truck. Thanks for asking."

"I've known you for quite awhile now, Mike. You're not the kind of guy who gets wasted and drives his truck off the road. So in the absence of a better explanation I'm going to have to accept that what you're telling me is true."

"Believe me, I couldn't make this stuff up."

"So, you went to this open service with Hayward looking for information on Ramon, just to see what it was like and this happens. Somebody at the compound wants you gone, which means you're getting too close to something, but what?"

"That's what I've been trying to figure out. Obviously, they — whoever "they" are — think I'm some type of threat. If they had just left well enough alone, we would have been none the wiser. As it is now, I've got to find out who attacked me and why."

"What's your next move?"

"I'm not sure. But, I did get a good look at the monk who was holding the incense burner and if nothing else, I can just drive out there and confront him. The direct approach is sometimes the best approach."

"Yeah, well, let me know how that goes. He might just try to blow you off and say it was the same incense they use at every service. Keep looking into Ramon. The police aren't breaking any land speed records and I have a feeling they're not taking this situation very seriously since it happened in Mexico. Oh, and Arrington's death is being handled as a typical drowning case, not suspicious. An autopsy was done. It'll be a couple of weeks before the results are released but it's pretty obvious that he drowned."

Arrington's death was a sad thing for surfing; he would be sorely missed. Paul said that with both Bobby and Arrington out of the running, there were only four guys who had a shot at the title: Sid Barrow, Butch Chu, Pietro Pradratz and Josh Phillips, who surfs for White Sand.

Paul's main competitors in the clothing industry sponsor all the other contending surfers. Paul said rumors were flying because of what had happened to two of the top-10 surfers in the last week and teams were hiring bodyguards to protect their surfers on the Pro Tour. Who could blame them? For me, a favor for a friend had turned into a full-on investigation that was certainly doing no good for my well-being — I'd been drugged by a deranged incense-wielding monk, had a rollover accident that totaled my truck, spent the night in jail, and now I had to deal with a DUI charge against me. I was definitely going to figure out who was responsible for this mess.

Wayne was at the gym when I got him on the phone and asked him to go with me to the Sycamore Grove compound. He picked me up within the hour and on the drive I went over what there was of my plan. It wasn't real complicated.

"I need to get in that monk's face."

At the Brotherhood's administrative office, I asked for Harvey Patel and after a short wait, Patel came out to the lobby and took us back to his office.

Patel is a small, neat man who always manages to project an attitude of calm deliberation. He's a prime example of a "morning shower person." My theory is that you can break the population down into two categories: people who get up in the morning and shower before work and people, like me, who go to work and then take a shower. Morning shower people usually remain clean throughout the day while evening shower people almost always get dirty. In my case, the shower theory is especially true since I'm usually up to my elbows in dirt at some point each day and I'm Irish — dirt is in my genes.

Wayne and I sat down and I related my story about attending last night's open service, my subsequent accident and my suspicions about the incense. I gave Patel the bare bones story without going into any of my curiosity about Ramon or his involvement with Bobby. I'd already decided that if Patel knew about what had happened in Mexico, I'd let him bring up the subject.

"Mike, I really don't know how you got such a strange idea. Why would anyone want to drug you?"

"I know it sounds crazy, Harvey. Believe me, I'm not accusing you, but something happened to me last night during that service. I can't remember ever being that out of touch with reality. I was hallucinating and my coordination was shot."

"That's certainly troubling but I can assure you that I've had no other reports or complaints from people who attended last night's open service."

If not for the fact that Patel knew me, I'm sure Wayne and I would have been escorted to the front gate at this point. Instead, Patel asked his assistant for information on the monks who had participated in the previous evening's ceremonies. While we waited, we discussed Patel's latest proposed development plans.

"We're making headway," he said. "You'll be my guy when construction planning gets underway. As a matter of fact, we're going in front of the Planning Commission tonight to try for a zoning variance."

Since I was sure that Patel was thinking I was nuts after this story I'd told him, I thought it was suspicious that he'd make mention of giving me work.

"Well, good luck. Variances are hard to get but I'm sure you're well prepared."

Patel smiled with appreciation at my compliment. His assistant returned with the information that six monks visiting from Santa Cruz had been the incense bearers at yesterday's service. All six were currently at meditation services in the chapel. Patel walked with us over to the chapel and we waited outside while he went in to talk with them.

He returned with five monks. My guy from the night before was not in the group. Upon questioning, they volunteered the missing monk's name: Brother Elias. When I described his looks, they all agreed that we were talking about the same guy.

"Brother Elias left the compound either late last night or early this morning with no notice or explanation," said Brother Simon, who seemed to be the spokesman for the group. "Elias is a new member of our congregation and as far as I know, he has no close ties to any member of the congregation or the Santa Cruz community. He's what you might call a loner. We were all supposed to stay together as a group so we were surprised to find him gone."

"Do you know Ramon?"

"Ramon meditated with us and he was friendly with Brother Elias," said Simon. "They spent a lot of time together since we arrived here in Encinitas."

I could see the Ramon discussion was causing some shifting feet within the group. Patel was paying close attention but that wasn't going to stop me. I figured it was time for one of those little white lies that doesn't hurt anyone but just might help me.

"You know, Ramon has worked for me in the past as a laborer on some projects and he never really struck me as a very religious person," I said using my most authoritative voice. "To put it mildly, he wasn't a very reliable worker."

That did the trick. "Neither one of those two seemed very interested in our studies," said Simon. "They always seemed to be off doing something else and when I asked them about it they just told me to mind my own business. I have to tell you I was shocked to have a fellow member talk to me like that and — "

Patel jumped in.

"Well, I think we've found out all we can about our missing Brother Elias. I'm very sorry about your unfortunate accident, Mike, but I really can't believe that one of our brothers was in any way responsible. I'm sorry he's not here to answer questions but we are a free and open congregation and people come and go as they please."

The monks from Santa Cruz took Patel's hint and retreated into the chapel. Patel began walking us back to the parking area.

"Why all the questions about Ramon? He wasn't even at last night's service." Apparently, Patel hadn't heard about the incident in Mexico, or he was doing a good job of playing dumb.

I figured, at this point, there was really no reason not to tell him about Ramon since he was a member of the PAB congregation. "Harvey, I hate to be the bearer of bad news but Wayne and I found Ramon dead two days ago in a camp outside Ensenada, Mexico."

"Well, that is a shock. How did he die?"

"He was murdered while in the company of Bobby Contraras. Bobby has no memory of what happened."

"I'll have to contact the family to offer condolences and make arrangements for a memorial service. I didn't know Ramon well but he was on his way to being a fine member of the Brotherhood."

He stopped at the entrance and shook my hand.

"Mike, I feel sure that you're going to find the reason behind what happened to you last night. Have you visited your doctor? Perhaps it was one of those mini-strokes you hear about. You do seem fine now, though, so let's be grateful for that."

I had no beef with Patel. The guy had always been a straight arrow with me as far as I knew. But I was convinced he had a crooked monk in his compound who was now conveniently gone.

Wayne was not real happy about being denied a chance to have a "conversation" with Brother Elias but I had a feeling we would be meeting somewhere down the road.

"There is something about Brother Elias's face," I said to Wayne as we got back into the car. "I feel like I have seen him before, like he's someone I've seen at the beach. I can't quite put my finger on it."

On the way back to the coast, I called Paul and told him our monk was in the wind and that I would let him know what the next move would be. Sometimes, when I try really hard to remember something, the memory seems to move further and further away and this was happening to me with my recognition of Brother Elias. I decided to just let it go for a little while and I hoped it would come to me.

Chapter 5

IN PURSUIT OF
THE MYSTERY MONK

I walked into the house with my usual greeting and received the usual silence in return. There was nothing on the answering machine or in my inbox that required my immediate attention. I also checked the fridge and was lucky enough to find the makings of a sandwich but there was a trip to the grocery store looming in my near future; the cupboards were downright bare. I settled in front of the television to watch one of my favorite shows while I ate.

A couple of years ago, Encinitas started televising its Planning Commission and City Council meetings and I love watching them both — they're usually better than almost anything else on TV. Plus, there are no commercials. People can get pretty worked up about small town politics and watching the interplay between citizens and the council members and commissioners is very entertaining. Many of the issues revolve around property rights and development issues and sometimes there's a great deal of money at stake.

This evening's Planning Commission agenda began with a couple who had been issued a permit to build a house, but once the house was almost complete, the city ordered that construction be stopped because the permit had been issued in error. Several neighbors came to the meeting to tell the commissioners to let the couple finish their house, so it seemed that the only people opposed to the project were the city staff. As I finished my sandwich and put my plate down, my eye caught the surfing magazine lying on the coffee table and right then I knew why Brother Elias's face was familiar to me. I had seen his face in one of my surfing mags.

But which one? I have issues of surfing magazines going back many years. When I finish reading an issue I usually put it on the top of the pile that I keep in my closet. When that pile gets big enough, it gets moved down to the basement. The current pile in my closet probably goes back about two years so I knew I could be in for a long search. I was fairly certain I would find his photo somewhere in that pile, but I didn't have a clue as to whether it was an advertisement or a photo layout. My only course of action was to look through each issue cover to cover.

I've always thought that intelligence alone is overrated. I place more trust in the virtues of hard work and persistence. All other things being equal, the person willing to work hardest will usually succeed. Looking through all these magazines was going to be a good test of my theory. As I flipped through the mags, I listened to the meeting. The Planning Commission ended up giving the couple a variance to complete work on the house. Well, score one for the idea that small-town government can actually work sometimes.

Ten mags down and 20 to go. The problem with doing a monotonous job is that your mind starts to wander and you lose concentration. I knew it would just take a second of distraction to miss that face so I urged myself to focus. Flip. Flip. Flip.

The next case came before the planning commissioners. A developer was — God forbid — threatening to cut down a pine tree. Poor schmuck. In Encinitas, community trees have assumed a position of paramount importance and builders had better remember to design around existing trees. The commission didn't even care what the developer's project looked like; they quickly sent him packing to find a way to save the tree.

Twenty mags down and 10 to go. I heard a familiar voice on the TV. I stopped turning pages and looked up to see Harvey Patel from the PAB. The room had filled with onlookers and Patel had a cadre of experts next to him. It looked like he was ready to do battle with the militant citizenry. I put the magazine down; this was going to be good. Each case usually starts out with a staff report and this particular planner sounded like an automaton as he droned on. Patel was asking for a zoning variance to do a mixed use project on one of the last remaining large residential parcels in Leucadia. I knew the staff report was going to take a while so I went back to the mag. Flip. Flip. Flip.

Patel and his team followed the report with their own 10-minute presentation stating why the project was great in every possible way and good for the community. Next up were the public comments. Twenty or so speakers each had three minutes to state their opinions on the project. Most were opposed to it. The public speakers are usually the most entertaining part of the meetings and Patel and his project sure took a beating.

The commissioners then weighed in with their highly intelligent questions. They quickly determined that there were no significant trees on the site. I put the mag down again. As a builder and an environmentalist, these types of cases interest me to no end. Plus, my eyes needed a rest. The zoning variance was denied. In Encinitas, all Planning Commission decisions can be appealed to the City Council so I knew this project would be back. I looked at magazines until I fell asleep on the couch.

* * * * *

Up early as usual for coffee and the all-important surf check, I was out the front door before I remembered I didn't have a car. The wind was picking up as I pedaled my bike to the beach and judging by the clouds on the horizon, a storm front from up north would move through soon. There would be no surf today.

I went home and dragged out more surf mags. I was on my second pot of coffee and running low on magazines before I struck gold. Brother Elias's face stared back at me from a wetsuit ad in an 25-month-old issue. I found the same ad with the same face in the two prior issues. I realized I had bought one of those wetsuits and that's probably why I had made the connection in the first place.

I walked down to the office and stopped by the gift shop to say hello to Claudia, who was busy selling tickets to a Japanese tourist couple on their way to San Diego.

"What happened to your forehead?" she asked. The bruise above my right eye had settled into beautiful shades of brown, purple and yellow.

I told her about my rollover accident, leaving out most of the gory details; she didn't need to know I was a jailbird. Toward the end of our conversation, she mentioned that the Brotherhood initiates were becoming a nuisance, bothering passengers waiting in the depot with their pamphlets. "Yesterday, I stopped two of them when they tried to go up the stairs to the offices."

I wondered if that was just a coincidence.

There were no business-related messages on the office answering machine. Just as well because I really had no time for such trivial things as earning money to pay bills and keep my ex happy. However, it finally dawned on me that my insurance agent might be interested in the fact that I had totaled my truck so I called his office and gave him the pertinent information.

There was a message from the attorney so I called him back. Bruce said that the drunk driving charge would probably be dropped because my blood sample had been negative for alcohol and there had been no presence of the typical drugs for which they usually screened.

It would be nice to know what type of drug was used to knock me out.

Bruce said he would request that my blood sample be kept, pending further investigation.

I called Paul to find out if could help me identify the monk in the Super Stretch Wetsuit ad. I stressed to Paul that this needed to be done very quietly as we didn't want to spook our prey.

"Got it," he said. "Super Stretch is a subsidiary of Third Reef Clothing, which is based in Hawaii. Third Reef is a major player in the industry. E-mail me a copy of the ad, magazine name, and issue date and I'll get right to work on it."

Paul went on to break things down in regards to the surf clothing industry while I took notes on the top five companies:

Company/Owner	Location	Sponsored Surfer
Ipenama/Pedro	Brazil	Pietro Pradratz
Third Reef/Sam Woods	Hawaii	Butch Chu
Koala/ Steve Reynolds	Australia	Sid Barrow
NorCal/Mark Henry	NorCal	Clyde Arrington
White Sand/Paul Maguire	SoCal	Bobby Contraras/ and Josh Philips

"Paul, let me run something by you — what about the possibility that one of the major surf clothing companies is responsible for Bobby's attack and maybe even Arrington's death?"

"I think you must have hit your head harder than you thought in that car accident the other night. I know the owners of all those companies and I can't believe that any of them could do anything like that. I thought you were looking at the PAB for some type of involvement."

"I think it's safe to assume that the Brotherhood is hiding something. I'm just throwing out an idea here about the clothing companies because greed is always a good motive. What's it worth to have the world's top surfer representing your company?"

Paul was quiet for a moment.

"You're talking big bucks, Mike. No doubt. Still, it just seems so far fetched. But I guess at this point we really can't rule anything out."

"They're having a memorial paddle out to honor Arrington up at Half Moon Bay in a couple of days. Can you get your clothing rep for that area to go by and see if he can pick up any information? You never know what might be useful."

"No problem, I'll make sure somebody is there. And I'll call you as soon as I get something on the monk."

After my conversation with Paul, I had some time on my hands so I decided to do some drafting. As a general contractor, I've looked at hundreds of sets of plans and one day I realized that I had absorbed enough knowledge to draw my own plans. I've always thought that architects, engineers and government employees operate using dog years as a measurement of time; one normal human day equals seven architects/engineer/government employee days. Now, I no longer have to wait for architects to finish my plans before I can submit for building permits. However, I still have to wait for engineers to perform, so I'm not entirely in the clear.

I pulled out the plans for a remodel/addition to my own house. I have no immediate desire to build but it'd be nice to have plans ready if and when I decide to do the work. Drafting can be very therapeutic because you can actually see the house coming together through myriad connection details until finally there's a completed whole plan that can be used to build the structure. It was a little hard to concentrate at first but eventually I got into the flow and made significant progress on the second floor plan and the roof deck. I also spent some time with my feet up on the desk doing the Highway 101 street scene stare and contemplating the events of the last few days.

The phone rang. Paul had one of his accountants call Super Stretch Wetsuits and act like White Sand had a W2 to send out to the same guy pictured in the ad but needed a current address for him. Super Stretch gave out a Mission Beach mailing address on Pismo Court and a name: John English.

Evening was coming on fast and it seemed best to do the monk search in daylight, so I put in a couple of more hours on my house plans and then headed home.

* * * * *

Wayne pulled up early the next morning and came in for some coffee. He thought it was odd that the monk had turned up in Mission Beach because it's near where I grew up. Mission Beach is close to San Diego, about 30 miles down the road from Encinitas. The address we had for the monk was in a neighborhood where I threw newspapers as a kid.

Mission Beach is basically a sand bar with the ocean on the west side, the bay on the east side and Mission Blvd. running down the center. The strip is probably one-quarter mile wide mile by two miles long. During the summer, the oceanfront boardwalk is a tangle of pedestrians, bikes and skaters and the white sandy beaches are packed with sun worshippers.

Back in the day, Mission Beach was an edgy place where drugs and alcohol flowed freely and the partying never stopped. Nowadays, many of the small beach cottages have been replaced by condos and the yuppies have settled in. But the area is still a formidable place to live. You have to be a certain personality type to call a tourist destination home. Mission Beach is equal parts late-night noise, tightly-packed housing and crowds for days but many people wouldn't trade life at the beach for anything.

Brother Elias's address was on the ocean side of Mission Blvd. Very small commercial lots line both sides of Mission Blvd., with the residential lots filling in between the street and the ocean and bay front. The houses front sidewalks, known as courts. Chances of finding a parking space in Mission Beach are, of course, slim to none so we pulled into one of the public lots on the bay side and formulated a game plan on the walk over.

Wayne went up to the house and returned with his report. The house was one of the last remaining small beach cottages on Pismo Court and had a parking area with a garage in the alley. "I knocked on the door and nobody answered." Wayne said. "The place is locked up tight."

We cut up to the boardwalk, which was practically empty this time of morning, and automatically started doing a surf check. The waves were small and glassy and several surfers were in the water in front of Pismo Court. There was a chance one of the surfers was our guy so we took a seat on the sea wall down the beach a short distance and waited.

The wind began to pick up and the surfers started to come in one by one. The last surfer walking up the beach looked like he could be our guy. He turned down the alley behind Pismo Court. Wayne walked down the boardwalk to loop around and I started down the alley, keeping my distance from the surfer. As I came around the corner of the house's garage, I came face-to-face with Brother Elias, the mystery monk. The garage door was open and he had just put up his board. His first instinct was to run but unfortunately for him at that moment, Wayne came through the side gate into the parking area. He flashed our monk a big smile. "Hey, buddy!"

Elias realized he couldn't escape so he walked over to an old beach chair in the garage and sat down, signaling his surrender. This would have been fine with me but Wayne had other ideas. While I was thinking about getting information, Wayne wanted revenge. He jerked the guy to his feet and planted two quick punches to his solar plexus, followed by a spinning back kick to the side of the head. I could tell Wayne pulled his punches but Elias was still flat on his back and out for the count.

I stood over him. He was average height, slim, early 30s with shoulder-length blonde hair. "He looks a lot different in a wetsuit than he did in a robe but that's the guy who drugged me with that incense."

It seemed like a good idea to close the garage door and conduct a quick search of the house while Elias finished his nap. The garage was connected to the small one-bedroom house; luckily there was nobody else home. I found mail addressed to Mr. and Mrs. Peter English as well as to John English, Elias's real name. Apparently his parents, who — judging by the clothes hanging in the closet — were not in residence, owned the house. The junior English's suitcase and backpack were on the bedroom floor. When I walked back into the garage, Junior was back in the beach chair with a look of abject horror on his face and his hands up in a gesture as if to ward off another assault from Wayne.

"Hey, Wayne, back off a second."

Our monk was terrified and most likely ready to answer some questions to save his own skin. He hadn't questioned our presence so I was certain he knew exactly who I was and had been totally blindsided by our appearance. His trail supposedly led to Santa Cruz not Mission Beach.

The main question I needed answered was who had given Junior his marching orders. I asked him that first because if he gave up the name he was off the hook psychologically since he had been "just following orders." Therefore, nothing was actually his fault. His answer surprised me.

Dede Betet is Harvey Patel's unobtrusive assistant at the Brotherhood compound.

"I didn't know anybody would get hurt." English's voice was close to a whine. "Betet told me to have Ramon get Bobby drunk, drug him and then take him to the survivalist camp in Mexico."

"Didn't you wonder what was going on?" Wayne asked.

"Betet said it was for the good of the Brotherhood and that I couldn't be told the details. Like I said before, I didn't know anybody would get hurt. Bottom line at the compound is that if someone like Betet asks you to do something you just do it, or you'll be out on the street the next day. My job was to supply Ramon with drugs and money and pass along Betet's instructions. I was supposed to stay here in Mission Beach until it was safe to come back."

According to English, Betet sent him to the Brotherhood compound in Santa Cruz weeks ago so that he wouldn't be traced back to Encinitas. Betet also supplied the drug that was used in the incense burner. "I don't know what the hell it was," he said. "But I was whacked out for hours, too."

When I pushed for more information, English said he had received orders from Betet only and he knew nothing about motive. He was just a mid-level cutout who did what he was told and would probably end up taking the fall for his superiors.

In his efforts to please, English volunteered that Betet was Indonesian and originally from one of the Balinese Brotherhood compounds.

I had already made a decision regarding English's fate, but after thinking about my crunched truck, I figured I'd freak him out for the hell of it. "My good friend Wayne and I won't tell anyone about our conversation," I said. "But we may need to talk to you again so don't even think about skipping town. We'll always be able to find you now that we know who your parents are. And one more thing, if you warn anyone at the PAB compound, and we find out about it, we'll turn you over to the sheriffs so fast it'll make your head spin."

On the drive back up the coast, I tried to consider all sides of the issue as far as what my next step should be. Wayne and I felt pretty good that we'd finally discovered some concrete information. Now we knew who had given the orders for Bobby's attack. We also knew there was a ruthless and devious mind at work trying to hide any involvement by the PAB. But we still didn't know why — what was the Brotherhood's motive and did it fit into my other theory about the surf clothing company turf war? There were still many unanswered questions, still a missing link in the chain that prevented us from understanding what was really going on. The Sheriff's department was running some type of investigation and maybe this would be a good time to let them take over.

I gave Paul a call and relayed all the new information we had uncovered from our Mission Beach monk. Wayne and I were pleased with what we'd accomplished so Paul's reaction was a little surprising.

"Tracking down that monk was good work. No, it was excellent work, but I want blood. I want someone to pay for Bobby. I want heads to roll. If we know this Dede Betet gave the orders and we can prove it, then I'm calling the Sheriff's detective and giving him all this information, names and addresses, everything. Let the cops figure out what's going on. "

"I have no problem with that, Paul. I was thinking the same thing."

"Good, I'm glad we agree. As soon as I'm off the phone with you, I'll make the call. I just hope the detective gets his ass in gear and moves before these guys go into hiding."

All things considered, this seemed like the best course of action. It would take the Sheriffs time to mobilize but I hoped they would be able to pick up both of our suspects before they tried to run. Plus, being basically a lazy person, I felt good about laying everything off on Paul. I knew he would keep my name out of things as much as possible and that he would make his best effort to get the Sheriffs to act quickly.

The time seemed right to visit Bobby so we stopped off at the hospital. Bobby was awake. He looked about five shades lighter than usual, his voice was weak and occasionally he would forget to finish his sentences. I've been in Bobby's position before so I tried to keep the conversation light but we did tell him about our recent conversation with John English. Bobby flashed us a big smile when Wayne described his punches and head kick.

"Don't worry, bro," Wayne said. "Everyone else connected to this B.S. will get the same."

71

Even though Bobby was obviously weak and drugged up, I still felt like I needed to ask him some questions. "Bobby, any idea why Dede Betet out at the Brotherhood compound would have put Ramon up to this?"

"No clue. I've never met him. I know PAB people but who doesn't? I've never been to a service. I can't explain it. I never did anything to those people."

"One more thing, Bobby. Do you remember anything else about your time in Mexico? Anything could help."

"Sorry, Mike. I know I let everyone down by falling off the wagon. Everything was going so good. Maybe it was the pressure of trying to win the title or maybe it was because I was starting to think that I really could pull it off."

"We don't have to get into that stuff right now, man; we can talk about that later. For now just tell me what you can about Mexico."

"I remember sitting around the campfire with Ramon and a bunch of other guys down at the migrant camp drinking beer and tequila, getting a buzz on. Somebody started passing around some weed. One thing led to another and pretty soon Ramon and I had come up with this great plan to go to Mexico. I remember Ramon driving my car and telling me to sit up straight and shaking me by the shoulder when we crossed the border. After that, it's a blur. Ramon must have put something in my drink. It's the only thing that makes any sense. Bits and pieces come back to me — being carried, lights in my eyes, hearing voices in another room — but nothing I can really put my finger on, nothing definite. This whole thing is like a nightmare."

Bobby was a naturally friendly and cheerful kid who had his share of problems with drugs and alcohol but his entire life centered on surfing and it was plain to see he was devastated.

"All right Bobby, just rest. Maybe you'll remember something else later. Right now your main job is to get better. Paul tells me the surgery went great and you'll be back in the water in no time. Just take it easy and don't worry, we're gonna find out what happened."

Several members of the Contraras family drifted in and out of the room. Bobby's sister, Maria, was there as well. She had barely left his side since he arrived. Maria walked into the hallway with us. She grabbed my hand and her eyes welled up with tears. "Thank you for bringing Bobby home," she said. "I'm doing what I can to keep his spirits up. I know it gives him a big boost to know you guys are fighting for him." She wiped her eyes and laughed. "Literally."

Maria raised Bobby after the death of their parents and had been his substitute mother. She was trying to be strong for his sake but it was not long before the tears began to flow again. We all sat together in the hallway while she got it out of her system.

Once back on the freeway, I became aware of how tightly I was gripping the steering wheel. "This thing with Bobby and Ramon has really gotten under my skin," I said to Wayne. "I think you're right about going after anyone who had anything to do with this mess." I could tell my words were music to Wayne's ears.

I pulled off the freeway a couple of exits before home so we could cut over to the coast and do a surf check, the same one I've been doing since junior high school.

Solana Beach is just south of Encinitas, and although it's also a small beach community, it has an entirely different feel. Unfortunately, the city allowed the bluff top overlooking the ocean to be turned into a Great Wall of condominiums, hence the nickname "So Long A Beach." Encinitas residents, me included, fought this type of development in Encinitas. Our bluff top is primarily medium density residential with a smattering of single-family residences.

Heading north on Highway 101, just as you leave Solana Beach and enter Encinitas, is a view I never get tired of — Cardiff Reef in the forefront and in the hazy distance, Dana Point. Recently, I've noticed signs of development just at the road's crest as you enter the view corridor. Once the view up the coast is lost we might as well be living in downtown L.A. But there's no stopping progress, right?

I saw right away that there was some type of swell — progressing lines of whitewater were coming in at Cardiff Reef. The adrenaline started to kick in and the anticipation began building. We pulled off Coast Highway into a parking area at the bottom of the hill and began watching sets of good six-foot waves rolling down the beach. Soon, Wayne and I were paddling out to the line-up. The waves were good and getting better but the word was out and there were quite a few people in the water. I found by moving out and over I could still manage to get a wave to myself.

A surfer, as a rule, is like any other athlete and is probably at his best in his teens or early 20s, when his reflexes and agility are at their peak. As a surfer grows older, he has to develop other faculties to compensate for diminishing skills because theoretically, the best surfers get the best waves. In my case, over the years I've developed the ability to outlast other surfers. The average surf session for most people is two to three hours but I can stay in the water for two to three times the average without a break.

The afternoon had turned overcast, with very little wind, and I was having trouble distinguishing between the water and the sky; everything had gone gray. I was sitting out and off to the south by myself, quietly staring at the horizon and waiting for the next set of waves to appear when I detected movement in my peripheral vision. A fin appeared, traveling straight at me. Thankfully, the fin belonged to a porpoise, part of a pod of six who were lazily making their way down the coast, searching for food and occasionally catching waves and making vertical leaps into the air. In years past, it was not uncommon to see pods numbering into the hundreds, but nowadays six to 10 are more common. A set of waves approached and several porpoises caught a wave and started gliding along the wave face just inches beneath the surface. As much as I wanted to catch that wave, the porpoise had the best position. I would have to wait for the next one.

I don't like to think about sharks when I'm surfing but seeing that porpoise fin heading straight for me reminded me of an extremely rare and tragic shark attack that recently took place nearby. A triathlete who was swimming with a group of others was attacked by a Great White and was so badly mauled, he bled to death on the beach before paramedics could help him. Shark attacks in Southern California are practically unheard of but Mother Nature can be a cruel mistress.

Off in the distance, I saw Wayne making motions towards the shore. He was headed in and would be back to get me around dusk. He knew me well enough to know I would surf until dark.

Chapter 6

GET READY

I walked in the door that night wet, cold, tired and hungry. Nevertheless, after a good five-hour surf session, life seemed pretty good. When you're in the water, it's possible to forget your problems. There are no telephone calls, e-mails or demanding clients — it's just you and the surf. However, reality was beginning to creep back into my consciousness so I called Paul.

He'd been in touch with the detective assigned to the case and had relayed all our information to him. The detective assured Paul that he would try to obtain arrest warrants for both Betet and English. I agreed to go to Paul's house the next afternoon so we could talk over the situation.

A really good night's sleep is a rare thing for me. Even after two years of being separated from Cathy, I still miss having that warm body in bed next to me. I think that's why I tend to spend a lot of nights on the couch. Also, my decades of working in construction have trained my internal clock. Job sites have to be open no later than 7:00 a.m. so no matter what time I fall asleep, a 5:30 a.m. wake-up is almost automatic seven days a week, 365 days a year with no time off for good behavior.

The morning was misty and foggy. I biked down to the beach, still pumped from the previous day's surf session. As I coasted down the hill, the shape of a stopped Amtrak freight train appeared through the fog. Trains run north and south through Encinitas on tracks parallel to Highway 101. Between commuter and freight trains there is a fair amount of rail traffic and the whistle warnings announcing their comings and goings are part of the city's soundtrack.

Trains only stop in the street intersections for two reasons. I turned down the next street crossing and pedaled over the tracks to the highway, wondering if the train was broken down or if it had hit someone.

The beautiful waves had disappeared overnight, which made me grateful I had surfed until dark and milked every last drop of energy out of the swell. I rode to my office, locked up my bike and walked in the back door of the bus station. Early mornings at the depot can be a scary proposition; you never know who or what you will run into. The night manager, Clive, was still on duty. He was probably hired more for his burly tattooed resemblance to a nightclub bouncer than for his office management skills but Clyde handles ticket sales, unruly drunks, and homeless people with the same quiet efficiency. I waved and asked about the train situation.

"The train took somebody out," Clive said. "They're doing the investigation and picking up the pieces."

I made a face. You'd think I'd be used to it by now because it's not uncommon for someone to get hit on the tracks. There's no separation between the tracks and the surrounding streets and people constantly take shortcuts across to get downtown and to the beach. Some people say when you're on the tracks, it's actually hard to hear the train coming. It's true that when a train is being pushed rather than pulled by a locomotive, it travels relatively quietly, but in my opinion it's quite difficult to be accidentally hit by a train. Most of time, it's probably a case of trainacide, if you will. The trains are extremely heavy and travel at speeds approaching 60 MPH. Collisions between people and trains are mostly always fatal and the aftermath can be traumatic for onlookers and especially for the train engineer, who doesn't have a chance in hell of stopping and can only watch as the train obliterates the person.

I headed to the office to spend a couple of hours organizing my life. Things were pretty quiet on the construction front. There were no clients eager to sign contracts to build their dream homes or nagging phone messages about dripping faucets or leaky roofs so I spent some time paying various bills then moved over to the drafting table and continued the design work on my future home remodel/addition.

Wayne announced his arrival with a train update and a stretching routine — he was decked out in his gui and headed to the gym for a Jui Jitsu workout. "Some guy was hit by a train. I've been watching them scrape him up from the tracks. He's scattered along a good quarter of a mile."

My daughter, Susan, is the editor of the local community paper so I gave her a call. She said that there was a reporter at the scene but still no name for the victim. I spent a few minutes updating her on all my adventures of the last week and asked her to call me as soon as there was an ID on the victim. Susan and I have been somewhat estranged since my wife and I separated. As with any marital breakup there is a tendency to assign blame. I blame my wife, my wife blames me and my daughter blames both of us. Because we're stubborn Irish bullheads, we're both waiting for the other to make the first move towards total reconciliation.

Susan called back a short time later with some unexpected news. The train victim was Dede Betet, Harvey Patel's administrative assistant.

"According to the train engineer, it was definitely a suicide. Betet stood on the tracks and waited for the train," she said. "Isn't that the last name you got from that monk yesterday? It's not the same guy is it?"

My mind was racing and I was a little slow on the uptake. Just a couple of days ago I'd seen Betet at Patel's office — when he was a living, breathing human being. Now he was gone forever, disintegrated by a train.

"Yes. That's the guy who gave the orders for the attack on Bobby. Wow, I can't believe it. He must have found out we were on to him and he just couldn't deal with the consequences of his actions."

Susan was just getting started with her questions but I noticed the time. I was running late. "Hey, I've gotta go — "

"This sounds pretty juicy, Dad. When can I run the story?"

"Now, hold on Suz. None of this stuff can be made public right now. We're still trying to piece together what happened and the police have an ongoing investigation. I promise nobody else will get the story but you have to wait. Okay?"

"Okay. But keep me posted. This story could really shake up our sleepy little seaside paradise where nothing exciting ever happens."

I thanked Susan, told her I loved her and that we should get together and talk things out.

My appointment with Paul was drawing near so I locked the office and started up the hill. I still needed to get the old Jaguar out of the garage, checked out, and warmed-up. I bought the 1965 Mark 11 3.8s many years ago from the original owner. She bought a new car and, for some reason, wanted me to have the old Jag. I had been doing work for this particular lady for quite a while and she knew whenever I walked by the car, I practically drooled with car lust. I was a starving college student with zero money but she told me to take the car with no money down and make payments when I could; a deal I could not refuse.

The four-door car has the full Jaguar hood ornament. The exterior is a very sleek light yellow and the interior is done in deep green leather and beautiful walnut. Jags are temperamental. While I've learned to do quite a bit of the maintenance on it myself, repairs are expensive. Regardless of the problem, the bill is always a thousand dollars, so naturally I try to avoid taking it in for service. That means the car spends most of the time in the garage but I still take her out for an occasional run and the trip to Paul's house was a good opportunity. I parked in the upper parking area away from the crowded driveway, but I was aware of the stares and thumbs up signs as I drove by. People love this car.

As soon as I sat down with Paul and Ellie, who looked to be in the same spot as the last time I dropped by, I sensed that Paul had the meeting totally mapped out from start to finish. I threw him off a bit by telling them about Dede Betet's trainacide.

"Brother Elias, aka John English, must have gone back on his word and warned Betet that he had confessed everything to me. Betet chose a very harsh and final solution to being exposed."

Both Paul and Ellie started talking excitedly but Paul was louder. "Well, either the bastard had a conscience or he just couldn't face discovery, disgrace and jail."

"Or he chose to die so he wouldn't have to face giving up names," said Ellie. "Maybe he was more scared of whoever's really in charge than anything else."

"That is a possibility," I said. "Maybe there are other people in the PAB whom he was trying to protect. In any case, I can't say I'm sorry he's dead. My only problem with it is now we may never know why he targeted Bobby."

Paul decided to call the Sheriff's detective in charge of Bobby's case. "You're right, it's possible that we might never find out what Betet was trying to accomplish. Maybe he was just a nutcase or it was some type of personal grudge. But it's supposed to be the Sheriffs' job to come up with those answers."

He waited impatiently while he was put on hold multiple times. Finally, he got through. "Have any arrests been made yet?"

There was a pause as he listened and then he put an abrupt end to the conversation. "Don't bother. In case you haven't heard, he committed suicide on the train tracks this morning."

Paul tossed his phone down on the coffee table. "They're still working on the warrants. He didn't know about the suicide. Can you believe that? But they've picked up John English. Of course, with Betet gone, that's probably going to lead to a dead end."

"Pun intended?" Ellie asked.

I smiled but Paul was already on to another topic, the real reason he asked me to meet. "So, Mike, how would you like to go to Indo with the team for the G-Land surf contest? And then to the Pipe contest in Hawaii?"

I was surprised by his request but it made sense. It was true that even though Betet was out of the picture, we couldn't be certain that there was no longer a threat to the top-10 surfers. I could keep one eye on Paul's contender, Josh, and at the same time attempt to track down information on Betet's Indonesian backround.

"I've made arrangements to have Josh looked after in Indo," Paul said. "But I'd feel better having you around for insurance, especially since you said Betet was originally from Indonesia."

Paul was the king of his clothing empire. He was used to making decisions and then having them carried out, no questions asked. He didn't much like being in a position of having to ask for things. When he asked me to find Bobby, he'd been able to do so on behalf of Bobby's sister. This time there was no way around a personal appeal. He produced an envelope, which I assumed contained a check, and leaned over the coffee table to hand it to me. "You'd be doing me a big favor."

I was deeply involved in this situation and more and more I was feeling like I wanted payback for Bobby and Ramon. I couldn't pass up the chance to look into Betet's background and to try to find an explanation why he gave orders that had such disastrous consequences.

"I'll do it with conditions. Once I arrive in Indo I'll make sure the team's okay but after that I'll need to go wherever I have to in order to run down leads. I can't be tied down. And I want to make my own travel arrangements."

Paul agreed.

We sat for a few more minutes, discussing the events of the past week that had completely disrupted our lives. Paul had spread the word far and wide in the surf clothing industry and competitive surfing community that he thought Arrington's death and Bobby's attack were both suspicious and possibly related. "I figured I'd throw it out there and see if anything sticks," he explained.

While Paul believed someone or some group was deliberately taking out surfing's elite, he still couldn't accept the theory that one of his fellow company owners may be responsible. We went over the list of his main business competitors: Pedro Valiz, Sam Woods, Steve Reynolds and Mark Henry.

"I'm not best friends with any of them," Paul said. "But I have a hard time thinking these guys are capable of murder."

Ellie leaned across her pile of paperwork and handed me her business card. "You saved Bobby's life." She put her hand on my arm and squeezed gently. Then she swiped her work into one pile, stuffed it into her bag and stood up. "The team's leaving Saturday. I'll be glad to have you with us. Watching these guys and trying to keep them out of trouble is a full-time job. I really don't need to be constantly looking over my shoulder worried about an attack on Josh."

Paul told me there was a copy of the team's itinerary in the envelope he gave me earlier, wished me good luck and asked me to keep in touch.

I was going to Bali, Island of the Gods.

Chapter 7

GET SET

During the drive back to the coast, I made a mental list of things to do before I left town. Most important was to get more information on Dede Betet. Upon arrival back at the house, I put in a call to Harvey Patel but his new assistant said he was not available so I asked for a call back.

I've done quite a bit of surf traveling; this would be my second trip to Indonesia. The Indonesian dry season is roughly equal to southern California's summer; the weather and water are very warm, the winds blow offshore and there are almost always waves. I packed T-shirts, shorts, flip-flops and one reasonably nice outfit, just in case.

I sent an e-mail to my friend, Steve Roper, whom I met on my last Indonesian trip to arrange for a room at his bungalows while I was in the Kuta Beach area. Next, I called Wayne and filled him in on the trip and asked him to check the office while I was gone. We also discussed the possibility of him flying over to meet me if I needed his help.

According to the White Sand team itinerary, the team was booked on a flight out of LAX Saturday at 1:00 a.m., arriving Denpasar Bali Sunday at 2:00 p.m. The team would stay in Kuta Beach two days and then leave for the contest site, G-Land, Wednesday morning and arrive later that day. I bought a ticket for the Monday at 1:00 a.m. flight so I'd have more time to wrap things up here in Encinitas but still be with the team in Kuta. So far, so good.

By early evening, I hadn't heard back from Patel.

My stomach was growling so I was forced to find something to eat. Although I've been a single guy for a while now, I still have not entirely mastered the art of feeding myself. However, I've come to realize that shopping at a grocery store can be an excellent idea. That way, when I go to the refrigerator my chances of finding food are greatly improved.

For years, the only retail stores I went into were the hardware store or the lumber yard, so learning to shop on a regular basis has been pretty painful. One of the first times I went into a grocery store after Cathy and I separated, the checker asked me, "Paper or plastic?" I had no idea what she was talking about so I told her I'd pay cash.

I've managed, though, to come up with a shopping strategy that works for me. I simply start at one end of the store and go up and down each aisle, scanning items and filling my cart. This method gets me through the process fairly quickly. A Zen-like trick that I use when shopping is to place my brain on autopilot and resign myself to the fact that I will be polite, patient and will not lose my temper. I use this altered state because even after the quickest shopping spree, I invariably get caught at the checkout stand behind the only person in the entire store who has to receive check-cashing authorization from corporate headquarters in Lower Slovobia. My daughter, the college graduate, says that my aversion to crowds and shopping is evidence that I was not properly socialized as a child. She's probably right. I have very few clear memories of my early feral childhood before the fourth grade — that's when I fell in love with the beautiful and alluring Sandy Finch, which seems to have brought me to my senses.

For now, I knew the fridge contained three beers, a jar of mayonnaise, and a questionable quart of milk. I didn't really have the time to go to the store. Besides, it didn't make sense to stock up right before leaving town. I was left with two dinner options: Pizza or pizza.

Pizza is the ultimate bachelor food. It requires no planning, can be easily obtained, doesn't need to be refrigerated and it's satisfying at any time of the day. For example, pizza makes for an excellent breakfast.

The closest pizza place is right down on Highway 101. They serve the best pie of the 10 or so Italian places in Old Encinitas. Plus, I can watch them prepare and cook my order while I have a seat at the counter and enjoy a beer. The place must employ half the surf rats in Encinitas, most of whom are also part-time students, so spending money there benefits them and the local economy. The owner, Peter, greets me by my first name and, best of all, he personally checks to make sure my pizza is cooked welldone. It may seem peculiar but I like it crisp around the edges.

I still had some trip preparations to take care of so I called in the order, waited about 10 minutes, then fired up the Jag and headed down the hill. What could be easier?

Not so fast. When I pulled open the front door, there was an ambush waiting — my ex and my daughter happened to be seated at the counter. There was an awkward moment while I figured out that retreat was impossible. We all knew I'd been "hiding out" to avoid dealing with personal issues.

The three of us took a booth for a nice family dinner and it turned out to be pleasant enough. Susan already knew most of what I'd been doing lately so we updated Cathy and discussed my trip to Bali. We had always been a close family when Susan was growing up. Only recently did I realize that Cathy and Susan are very close, not only as mother and daughter but also as friends and confidantes. Susan is truly her mother's daughter.

Although I am a native Encinitian, I descended from Irish-American stock, which my name gives away immediately: Michael James Fitzpatrick Malone. My grandparents came from Ireland to the east coast. My parents moved west just like many other military families during World War II. The Irish are predisposed to be argumentative, stubborn and moody, causing a great deal of family problems. My mother and sister have both been divorced three times and are currently single. Both my brothers have each divorced twice. One is still single and the other has remarried. My siblings and my mother are all are charter members of Alcoholics Anonymous. In other words we are a typical Irish-American family.

When my daughter came along, I promised myself that I would provide her with a good stable home life, primarily for her overall well-being but also to prove that somebody from a broken home, times three, could have a successful family. Susan had a happy and stable childhood. She turned out fine, obtained an excellent education along the way, with a BA and MA in Journalism, and is in a long-term relationship. Yet her Irish genes handicap her and I can tell she is still not completely happy.

As we finished dinner, Cathy took a few minutes to complain about not getting enough money to keep up with the rising cost of living. I told her I would work harder and try to do better. That seemed to make her happy and we parted friends. Just in case, I reminded them where my important papers were kept if anything should happen to me on my impending trip.

On my way out the door, I put a big tip into the jar. I have a soft spot for surf rats having spent my own youth hanging out at the beach and the local surf shop.

* * * * *

Up at my usual time drinking coffee and watching the Weather Channel, I checked the online surf forecast but the only way to know for sure was to ride down and take a look.

Of course, the Internet has had a tremendous impact on the sport of surfing. Surf cams stream live pictures of many beaches so a drive to the beach can be replaced by a session of surfing the web. But while online surf forecasts are easily accessed, they have led to a strange phenomenon, which I refer to as the "phantom Internet swell." Hordes of surfers will show up like lemmings at the beach in the morning because a swell was predicted online and they'll paddle out regardless of whether a swell has actually arrived. Even the most accurate surf forecasters frequently miss the mark so a drive to the beach is still the best method of doing a surf check.

I've always believed that surfers, in general, are optimists. Why else would they go to the beach every day expecting to find good waves? It's kind of like life; you hope for the best, but sometimes you end up disappointed and asking "Why do I do this to myself?"

A surfer is always looking for that one magic morning when swell, tide and weather all come together to produce epic waves. Surfers constantly complain to each other about bad surf conditions. They will stand around for hours finding different ways to voice the same complaint. It's easy to become discouraged with daily surf checks but it's a rule that the first morning you decide to sleep in, a swell will miraculously appear out of nowhere. Then, the next day at the beach you'll have to endure the infamous, "You should have been here yesterday, you really missed it."

For me, there has to be a chance of catching at least a few good waves before I will venture out into the water. There is, however, something called "the desperation level," meaning that the longer I've been unable to go surfing the more desperate I become. Sometimes you just go out to "get wet." There is one surfer in central California who holds the record, I believe, for surfing every day for 13 years. Obviously, that guy is not very particular.

After prolonged periods of surfing dry spells, a common ailment I've noticed in others and myself is "surf withdrawal," as evidenced by being argumentative and generally irritable. The only known cure is one good surf session. I'm not sure of the exact ratio, but one good day of surf makes up quickly for all those disappointing trips to the beach. It truly is an addiction, but a good addiction.

The waves were small and not very good but as the tide came up there was a chance of better surf later in the morning. John Hayward was also doing the surf check. I gradually brought up the subject of Dede Betet's tragic accident. If John knew it had been a suicide, he wasn't letting on but he did say everyone at the compound was freaked out by his death. Talking to John was always an adventure. He sometimes answered questions but, just as often, he brought up a totally unrelated subject or he did not respond at all. I decided to use the direct approach.

"John, did you notice any difference in the way Betet had been acting lately?" I guess that's the question that always gets asked when a person commits suicide.

He didn't say anything for a long few moments. I was just about ready to give up when he started talking.

"Dede was in administration so I really didn't see him that much. He lived at the compound and spent most of his time behind a desk. I remember seeing him talking to Brother Elias a couple of times, which was weird because Elias was new and Dede was high up. He was Harvey's right hand man, you know? I guess he killed himself but nobody at the compound is talking about it like that. Killing yourself is against the teachings. But maybe since

Dede's from Indonesia, they have a different ruling on that."

For John, this was a virtual torrent of information and it did contain some useful nuggets. "Do you happen to know where he was from in Indo? I'm just curious."

"No, I don't think I ever heard anybody talk about it, but I can try and find out if you want."

"Yeah, John, I'd appreciate it if you could find out. Hey, I think I'm gonna go for a quick surf. See you later."

The tide had started to push in and the waves were beginning to look fun so I rode home, loaded my board onto my bike racks and headed back down to the beach. During the crowded summer months, the bike racks are the only way to go. I can just pull up to the beach and get in the water while everyone else is looking for a parking place.

While sitting outside waiting for a wave, it suddenly occurred to me that I would need a picture of Betet to have handy while searching into his past. The PAB has a Visitor Center in downtown on Highway 101. I figured the center would provide my best chance to obtain a picture of Betet before leaving for Bali.

It looked like I would be heading to the center sooner rather than later. Even though I had made my usual hike down the beach, the crowd was gradually working its way down towards me and the tide was also coming in so there were fewer waves available. Surfing can get really competitive and on a crowded day things can degenerate quickly. If certain rules and procedures aren't followed, there can be chaos in the water.

Impulse control is very important in surfing, as usually there is very little time to make a decision on whether to paddle into a wave or to let it pass. Looking up and seeing a beautiful wave coming toward you can tempt even the most civilized and courteous surfer. That's where impulse control comes into play. Just because you see a wave and want the wave doesn't mean you can have the wave. This is the same lesson we teach toddlers in preschool to avoid playground squabbles. We all have impulses. Fortunately, we usually do not act on all of them but instead consider the consequences and proceed accordingly.

Surfing etiquette requires that the person who paddles into the wave first and is closest to the breaking part of the wave is entitled to surf that wave without interference from others. When someone suffering from Surfer Impulse Control Disorder (SICD) disregards standard surfing practices and takes off in front of someone who is already up and riding, it is considered very rude and such action can bring negative consequences.

The first and most obvious outcome is that the "injured" party can simply forget to stop and literally run the other person over. Unfortunately, this happens frequently. There are also shouting matches and physical altercations. I've even seen one person pick up his small surfboard and use it like a tomahawk against his opponent. Thankfully, this seedy side of surfing is not the norm and people mostly manage to coexist and enjoy the ocean.

When I learned to surf, there were older guys in the water who made sure the rules were followed. More often than not, their oversight included direct physical punishment. Or the offender was simply kicked out of the water and told to leave the beach. Our local crew consisted of at least 10 guys in the water and probably as many on the beach at any given time and if there was a problem in the water, the offender was dealt with quickly. One offense that was never tolerated was someone bullying one of the little local kids — known as "grommets" — who were totally unable to defend themselves from larger surfers.

Back in the day, the enforcement system worked very well; it imposed a type of order on an otherwise ungovernable situation. Now, however, if you even touch another surfer you are subject to arrest and criminal as well as civil litigation.

There's one incident I will always remember from my grommet days. I had just come in from surfing when this big ugly pissed-off guy got right in my face. A few minutes before, I had run him over when I could have avoided him and it was time to pay the piper.

In those days, the beach closed for surfing daily at 11:00 a.m. so that swimmers could have exclusive use of the ocean. The beach closures were a source of contention between surfers and lifeguards. "Lifeguard wars" were almost daily occurrences where angry and frustrated lifeguards charged into the water in pursuit of surfers who refused to obey the 11:00 a.m. closure. I saw the big ugly pissed-off guy on the beach waiting for me so I stayed in the water as long as possible but the unavoidable moment of truth arrived.

Bruiser caught up to me in the street as I was trying to escape and his right arm was flexing when I heard someone ask, "Is there a problem here?" From the other side of the street someone else called out, offering me help. The good Samaritans, Gary Cook and Bob Reaman, were both local heroes and surfing legends. They saved my 70-pound grommet butt from a severe beating. Cook was known as the "King of Crystal Pier." He was a masterful surfer and was one of the most unappreciated surfers of his era.

There are many current-day surfers who have never learned proper surfing manners, in large part because of the breakdown in "local enforcement procedures."

On this particular surf day, I couldn't help but notice one rather large and burly violator of accepted surfing protocol. He was terrorizing the local groms who could only paddle away, give him dirty looks and offer backhanded comments. On my next wave, I was not surprised to see this large idiot drop in on the wave in front of me so I gave him the two hands on the back shove-off. Naturally, when he came to the surface he was surprised and angry. As I paddled back out, I gave him a quick rundown of the "No Drop-in Rule," which I doubt very much he understood given his Neanderthal mentality. But it sure made the local "groms" happy.

Physical violence is rare in the southern California surf scene but it's best to be prepared and I steeled myself for a tussle. However, this particular surfer decided it was best to paddle away, muttering under his breath. I stayed out for a while longer but conditions were deteriorating and the wind was picking up. So having done my small part to restore a semblance of order to the surfing lineup through the practice of "local enforcement," I rode my next wave to the beach.

* * * * *

The bike ride down the hill to the beach is a snap. The ride back up the hill, however, is not so nice. After a quick shower I was on my way back down the hill to the PAB Visitor Center.

The center is a destination point for visitors from around the world. As I cruised the aisles, I recognized German, Dutch and Japanese being spoken as well as several other languages I couldn't identify. There were rows upon rows of books and pamphlets and after about 30 minutes of looking for a photo of Betet, I was starting to get discouraged. I headed to the front desk to make inquires but on the way I saw a large display of free brochures. On the back cover of one of them was a group photo of the Sycamore Grove administrative staff posed in front of the courtyard fountain. Dede Betet could be seen clearly in the front row seated next to Harvey Patel. Bingo.

Next, I rode down to the print shop and had them crop and enlarge the middle portion of the picture and got several copies made for distribution. When I returned to the house, I again called the Sycamore Grove compound and was told Patel was on a weekend retreat because of the events of the last week and could not be disturbed. I was starting to get the feeling that Patel did not want to talk to me.

Paul called and told me, "My clothing representative went to the memorial paddle out for Arrington and the only thing he picked up was the same info Josh already told us; that Arrington had to run over to his truck to chase away a bunch of PAB members."

"You know, Paul, it really wouldn't have been that hard for one of those PAB guys to tamper with Arrington's equipment. A loose connection or a strategically placed nick in his surf leash could have led to his drowning."

"It's possible, but with no witnesses or confessions, Arrington's death will go down as an accidental drowning."

I went over my Indo itinerary with Paul and asked him to follow-up with Patel.

"Patel has been ducking my calls but keep after him since he is one of the few people I know who can give us any info on Betet. His new office assistant is telling me he is on a retreat until Monday."

We agreed to talk again mid-week or thereabouts.

By evening, I still had not gotten around to grocery shopping so I was forced to walk back down the hill for a quick and easy meal. Downtown was busy with cars backed up at the lights and pedestrians cruising the sidewalks checking out the eateries and bars. I wandered over to the small Mexican take-out run by the grandmother I've nicknamed "Mamacita." She has to stand on a box just to see over the counter. It's a family business and at one time or another, the whole extended family can be found either working the counter, cooking or cleaning the outside eating area. I sat at one of the outside tables and enjoyed some people-watching along with my chile relleno and taco combination plate.

Across Highway 101 at the La Paloma Theater, people were lined up around the block for the premiere of a new surf movie. La Paloma — meaning "the dove" in Spanish — is one of the most important landmarks in Encinitas. Built in 1927, the building is a Spanish colonial design with a three-story square tower on the north end answered by a church-like pitched roof of equal height on the south side. A lower two-story mansard roof covered with the traditional red clay "S" tiles connects the two sides. Various recesses, projections and black wrought iron railings add visual interest and play well against the building's stark white stucco walls. At night, the brightly illuminated marquee casts a glow that extends to the businesses on either side of the theater, as if bringing the entire block under La Paloma's wing.

It used to be that almost all the small coastal towns had a local theater but these days only a few remain. I wondered how many of the fathers of those blonde-headed surf rats across the street had waited in a similar line on a busy Saturday night. The theater is part of the fabric of the community and I'm grateful the owners have been able to keep the doors open all these years.

After dinner, I made a quick stop at the office. There were the usual cast of characters hanging at the bus station both inside and out — street people, druggies, normal citizens in transit, even a couple of PAB initiates in shirts and ties were working the crowd. While traversing the lobby area, I caught Clive's eye. He pointed to one of the rear benches against the wall. John Hayward was sitting there, looking at a magazine. I invited him up to the office.

"Have a seat."

I handed him a can of soda from the mini-fridge and grabbed one for myself.

"Thanks. I spent most of today at the compound. Between the Sheriffs asking about Bobby and everyone talking about Dede, it was not its usual state of peacefulness."

John took a swig of soda.

"Dede was originally from Bali in Indonesia where he had been a member of the PAB for a long time. He'd been over here on a work visa for the past four or five months. That's all I could find out. Does that help you?"

I assured him it did and then I changed the subject. I didn't want to stress John out. He was a good guy who had a lot to deal with. I was also aware the John could just as easily be a source of information about me for any interested parties at the PAB compound. We talked about surf for a while and then I walked him downstairs. As we said goodbye, he remembered something: "The Brotherhood has two compounds in Bali. The main temple is in town and there is a smaller one out in the country somewhere." We shook hands and said good night.

On the way home I dropped into the Saloon and had a couple of drinks. I shot the breeze with a few of the locals and caught the end of the Padres baseball game. Over the years, I've gone through different phases of enthusiasm for the Padres. They've disappointed me so many times. Padres fans have had some high points — the clutch hits by Curt Bevaqua and Steve Garvey; Tony Gywnn's classy career and making it to the World Series in 1998; but they've been few and far between. The final disappointment that caused me to lose interest in baseball was in 1994 when a labor dispute concerning money and benefits prematurely ended the season. That year, Tony Gywnn was hitting over .400 (the first player to do so since Ted Williams in 1941) and the dispute put an end to his hitting streak. I still root for the home team but baseball has never been the same for me. By no means would I put Padres fans in the same league as Chicago Cubs fans when you compare agonizing defeats and general suffering, but we can never seem to put that one magic season together.

It was late when I got home. I started to finish packing but was soon on the couch falling asleep while watching some idiot on TV solve a gruesome murder.

Chapter 8

GO TO INDO

I woke up excited about my impending trip to Bali. I called the airport shuttle and confirmed my pick-up time and then finished packing and tied up some loose ends, like prepaying bills and watering the yard. I also did some more research on the PAB. The reach of the organization was impressive — the Brotherhood has temples and compounds around the world, with the Bali headquarters located in the city of Ubud. My attempts to find more Internet information on Betet were a washout.

The shuttle arrived at 9:00 p.m. and the drive to LA went quickly. I handed the driver a good tip after he unloaded my gear curbside in front of the China Airways departure area. I headed for the check-in counter and was promptly told I was in the wrong place. I needed to be at China Airlines, which was located about one–half mile from my current location. Not a good way to start a trip.

I commandeered a luggage carrier, threw my duffel bag on and carefully balancing my boards on top, began the slow push to the correct check-in counter. I was still grumbling about two airlines having names so similar when I finally reached China Airlines. The counter person laughed and said that mix-up happened all the time.

Moving through airports with surfboards — I had two in one bag — is awkward. You have to be careful not to run into people and there's never enough room in the lines to maneuver. I always breathe a sigh of relief when I'm able to get rid of the surfboards and stop feeling like I'm trying to stuff a size 12 foot into a size six shoe.

The flight from LA to Bali is grueling. Total air travel time is about 18 hours, with a layover in Taiwan. The flight was full, so my hopes of stretching out were dashed. Almost all the passengers were Taiwanese returning to their country, so I immediately got that old familiar feeling of being the strange-looking visitor from another country. Between my i-Pod stocked with classic rock, my books and the built-in TV screen, I managed to idle away the time but any way you look at it, 13 straight hours in the air seems like an eternity. I usually read while watching TV so that if one goes stale, I can concentrate on the other — anything to avoid the dreaded enemy: boredom. I'm currently reading the Bolitho series of 18th century seafaring adventures by Douglas Reeman. Recently, I finished all the historical fiction of CS Forrester as well as Patrick O'Brian, Bernard Cornwell and George Macdonald Fraser. On a trip to the local library one Sunday afternoon, I asked the librarian where I could find some of my favorite historical fiction. She directed me to the young adult section. Seems my literary taste, according to the librarian, runs to the simplistic. But for me, it's all about enjoyable escapism and I cannot remember the last time I read a nonfiction book. My bookshelves are also packed with mystery, spy and detective novels. Sherlock Holmes, George Smiley, Hercules Poiret, Dave Robicheaux and Easy Rawlins are among my literary heroes.

During the layover in Taiwan, I managed to get lost in the big modern terminal. It was necessary to take a shuttle train from one end of the terminal to another and since none of the announcements were in English, I ended up sitting patiently in the wrong area for about an hour. I finally realized my mistake and retraced my way back to a hub where several walkways took off in different directions. Good thing I had four hours between flights. I did my best "lost tourist" routine and finally managed to pick the correct route to the Bali departure gate. Man, it was stressful. To help get my blood pressure back under control, I went into a bathroom to splash some cold water on my face. The bathroom was white-tiled and immaculate but I was shocked to see that someone had stolen the toilet. Actually, the hole where the toilet would have sat on the floor was also nicely tiled. Later, I was informed that this setup is known as a "squatty potty" and is considered perfectly normal in certain parts of the world. Well, I try to learn something new every day.

The flight out from Taiwan was not so crowded. It's funny how those empty seats seem to give the appearance of having more room; even breathing seems easier. I must have dozed off because when I regained my senses, the engines were decelerating and changing pitch; the pilots were preparing for landing. I'm really not a very good air traveler. I hate crowds and detest being cooped up but I can usually manage to maintain the outward appearance of a sane and rational person until I get to the main terminal and then all my instincts tell me to run. Arriving in a foreign country can be particularly horrible because of all the porters and cab drivers that swarm around the shell-shocked, jet-lagged travelers like sharks going after chum. It ain't pretty. I almost managed to avoid that scene but just before I got to my bag, three porters swooped in and each grabbed a corner of it. They carried it 30 feet, put it down and then extended their hands for a tip; all the while eyeballing their next victim.

My friend, Steve Roper, had replied to my e-mail saying he would pick me up at the airport. But he was nowhere in sight so I got my bags and boards together and headed for the exit, where there would surely be a cab, as quickly as I could. The Denpasar terminal is not a big operation and this rush hour of flight arrivals was causing quite a commotion. I couldn't wait to get out of there. From out of a seething mass of humanity, a bright red-haired local approached and gestured to take my board bag.

"Mike? I'm Denzu. Steve's business partner."

I was rescued.

Indonesians drive on the left-hand side of narrow congested roads. Driving here is not for the faint of heart. I made some polite conversation with Denzu but he knew what I really wanted to talk about.

"Surf's been between four and five feet with good shape."

We headed for Uluwatu on the Bukit Peninsula. Steve's group of rental bungalows are built around a courtyard, pool and central gathering and eating area. The houses and property are nice but their location is remarkable. You can stand on the grounds and see the swells as they pulsate into the legendary surf spot of Uluwatu. Plus, there's a stairway that winds down directly to the beach. When I found out I was to stay in the three-story tall Tower Room, my hectic travel became a distant memory. I went up to the top floor immediately and took in the fantastic views up and down the coastline. On my walk down for a surf check, I saw Steve. On my last trip, he and I bonded after I found out he's also from San Diego and that we have some mutual acquaintances. I thanked him for the airport pick-up and we agreed to meet later.

Surfing a Southern California beach break is nothing like surfing an Indonesian reef. The reef is more powerful by a magnitude of 10. Just getting to the surf is totally different. In Southern California you walk across a sandy beach while in Indonesia, at low tide you may have to walk across a quarter-mile of shallow reefy water to get to a point where you can paddle out.

The tide was low and the waves were small and not worth surfing so I just took a stroll, venturing out onto the reef just to get the feel of the place again. Then I walked back up to Ulu, as the locals call it. Ulu is a whole little happening community of restaurants, surf shops, souvenir booths, massage areas, restaurants and small markets known as warungs, all offering seats where you can rest and watch the perfect lefts peel down the point. I bought a soda and sat awhile, admiring the view.

Back at my Tower Room, I took a long hot shower and changed my clothes. Then I walked over to the office area and, after quite a bit of translation and questions and answers, managed to get one of the girls to call the Melasti Beach Bungalows, where Ellie McPherson and the team were staying. Ellie welcomed me to Bali and invited me to an awards ceremony dinner with all the surf team members at the Melasti. I agreed to meet her at the bar beforehand so we could have a few minutes to talk alone. I arranged for a cab to pick me up at 7:30 p.m. and requested a wake up call, just in case. As soon as I sat down on the couch in my room, I entered a blissful state of unconsciousness — the day I lost flying from California to Indonesia had caught up to me. It was a good thing I asked for the wake up call. I felt groggy but the hot and then cold shower did the trick.

When the cab arrived, I recognized its number, 261 as the same cab I used on my last trip. I tried to impress the driver with one of my six Indonesian phrases.

"Ken ken bli bagus" means "How are you, bro?"

I asked about Wayan, who was the driver on my last trip. I was told he'd be working the next day. Cabbies in Bali are very familiar with surfers. Most cabs have surf racks and drivers pick up and drop off at all the local breaks.

Bali is totally geared toward tourism, almost to a ridiculous extent. Just walking down the street in downtown Kuta, you can be offered just about any personal service imaginable — from full body massages to nose and ear hair clipping. The tourist industry was badly hurt as a result of the terrorist bombing in 2002 and security in the form of fencing, gates, and guards is now very noticeable. But the one thing that hasn't changed is the Kuta Beach area is still party central. Driving to the Melasti took us straight through Kuta and the sidewalks and streets were packed. Motor cycles are very popular in Bali and they're constantly dodging in and out of the thick traffic.

I ended up at a corner table in the bar area, which was actually a patio adjoining the pool. I ordered two big tropical drinks complete with umbrellas. My drink was halfway gone by the time Ellie walked up to the table. She had gone native, sporting a colorful sarong that highlighted her tanned features and long blonde hair.

As the White Sand Team manager, Ellie spends a great deal of her time babysitting. The average age of the team members is around 22 and the riders are constantly looking for ways to get into trouble. Josh Phillips was very unhappy that he'd been virtually under guard since his arrival in Bali. Ellie said the entire team was leaving for the contest site early in the morning by boat and that while the rest of the team would be allowed out tonight, Josh was confined to quarters. He was being kept company by two local clothing representatives.

We talked about the contest. Access to the famous surfing destination of G-Land is mainly by boat and during the contest anyone arriving has to be either on the organizers' or surf camp staff's approved list or they'll be turned away. Ellie and I agreed that if Josh was targeted for attack it would happen in Bali.

Out of the corner of my eye, I saw someone familiar approaching our table but I couldn't put a name to the face.

"Hey there, Pedro," Ellie introduced me as a friend from Encinitas to Pedro Valiz, a Brazilian and president of Ipenama Clothing. We talked briefly about the contest and he wished Ellie luck and said he would see us at dinner. As soon as he was out of earshot, Ellie started tearing him apart.

"Oh God, he just makes my skin crawl," she said. "He's so underhanded. Man, he'll do anything to win. I've seen his riders intimidate people in the water and interfere with waves and it all goes back to him."

Sounds like someone to keep an eye on.

I told Ellie my plans for the next day included a trip to the PAB headquarters in Ubud to look for information on the recently deceased Dede Betet. We finished our drinks and went into the dining room where the professional surfers, their sponsors, and assorted local dignitaries and guests were being seated. Dinner was eaten to the accompaniment of an awards ceremony, which was handled nicely by a fast-talking emcee. The awards were mostly humanitarian honors given to both companies and deserving individuals. Having been around surfing all my life, I've been to many similar functions and they're usually a drunken good time, but the atmosphere in this room was subdued and oddly formal. About halfway through the main course, Ellie explained the tension: Word was that the point count for the number-one surfer slot, after the elimination of Bobby and Arrington, was now very close between Brazil, the Aussies, the Hawaiians, and of course, Josh.

After dinner, I went with Ellie, Josh and the two clothing reps back to Josh's suite. He was not happy about being "locked-up," but after getting the X-box running, he seemed resigned to his fate.

The rest of the team was, of course, going to do the town. After repeated invitations, I decided to go along.

Downtown Kuta was throbbing with people, lights, noise, confusion and music. It's taken me about 15 years to figure out that although I'm Irish, I can't drink worth a damn and so I limit my alcohol consumption to beer. Plus, I only drink on the weekends. It may sound weird but it works for me. I like looking forward to that brewski come Friday night.

On this Monday evening, I was one of the few sober people thronging the downtown area. Watching drunks can be quite entertaining; sometimes it's like watching a car wreck in slow motion. There were about 15 people in our group and we hopped from one bar and disco to another, eventually ending up at Joyo's, which seemed to be the epicenter of the Kuta Beach insanity. Naturally, the Australians had taken over the club and were in full party mode, crash dancing and even threatening to join in with the band on stage. I have a soft spot for Australians. Maybe it's because we always had Aussies at our local beach when I was a kid. They'd travel over and visit us and then some of our crew would go over and visit them; an unofficial exchange program. It's always seemed to me that Australians are a good-hearted people and definitely know how to enjoy themselves. They're a little rough around the edges, maybe, but then so am I.

Two of my high school buddies went to visit Australia and decided to stay. One comes back once in awhile to visit and work but he always goes back to Australia. My other friend, Vince Barrow, went over and I never saw him again. Years later, I started hearing about a young Aussie surf phenom, Sid Barrow, Vince's son. Nowadays, Sid is sponsored by Koala Clothing and is winning contest after contest.

I could see him sitting with his mates at a table near the dance floor, enjoying the insanity at Joyo's. It is a small world.

Most of the Aussies know Ellie and the White Sand surfers so they welcomed us with a few rounds of drinks for our tables. After a while, I started sending them rounds of tequila shooters. "Just to make sure they all felt really lousy in the morning," I told Ellie before she hit the dance floor.

She brought back one of the Aussies to our table and I mentioned to him that I'd known Sid Barrows' father back in the States. Soon, Sid, accompanied by Koala Clothing Owner Steve Reynolds, came over. I asked Sid to say hello to his dad for me and he gave me a big smile and shook my hand. I felt like I was receiving the official Australian seal of approval.

Sid returned to his mates but Steve sat down and we talked about the upcoming contests and the close race for the number one slot. Steve came on like a typical good-natured and down-to-earth Aussie. You'd never know that he was a multimillionaire clothing company magnate. In Australia, surfing is a huge sport much like football or baseball in the US and successful surfing pros are akin to national heroes. I managed to get in a few words with Steve about the potential threat to Sid and the other point leaders. He looked at me kind of funny, as if I was kidding around and then pointed over his shoulder towards the group surrounding Sid at his table. He was right; Sid was as safe here as if he had a Secret Service detail to protect him. Australians were among the first to surf Bali and to many of the Aussie surfers, it's like a second home. Steve bought a round for the table and then excused himself.

One by one, our crew started heading for the door so Ellie and I decided to leave as well. In Bali, a quick way to grab a ride is to flag down one of the funny-looking pony carts that carries people up and down the main road.

We headed back to the Melasti, listening to the sound of hooves hitting the pavement amongst the whine of motorcycles and taxis.

* * * * *

At the hotel, we checked on Josh and everything was cool. The two clothing reps on protection detail had the night divided into shifts and they said that Josh had gone to bed.

Ellie and I did the same, which was a great way to end the evening. I was sure it was a casual thing but it was exciting to go with the flow and the flow with Ellie had turned into a torrent. Afterward, I contemplated my situation. The lovemaking had seemed mutually satisfactory, judging by the noise level, but I was out of practice since my separation so just to make sure we were "good," I attempted to make small talk. A loud banging at the door cut off my considerable efforts.

I laid back and enjoyed the view as Ellie went to the door and opened it a crack. She shut it again quickly and started throwing her clothes back on.

"Josh is gone."

According to the clothing reps, Josh had flown the coop by crossing from his room's balcony over to the next one and then dropping to the ground-floor walkway.

We took a cab to Joyo's, where he was surely headed. We spotted him as soon as we walked in the door. He was with the Aussie contingent, which was still going strong. Josh saw us as well but chose to ignore us so Ellie and I found a table and sent the clothing guys over to talk to him. The group couldn't go on drinking for much longer — it was past 2:00 a.m. and they all had to leave for G-Land in the morning so we waited it out. At the rate Josh was putting away the boilermakers, we'd probably have to carry him out feet first. Eventually, with a little help from the reps, Josh started unsteadily in our direction.

The street was much quieter now. As I looked for a taxi, I heard Josh head for the nearest alley to discharge excess alcohol. Ellie grabbed my arm and when I looked at her she was staring at a group of locals on motorbikes who were pulling up en masse across the street. This seemed odd because most people were headed home at this time of the morning. One of the riders pointed in our direction and then I saw another group walking towards us on the sidewalk about one-half block down on our side of the street. I moved quickly to pull Josh out of the alley. I was hoping to get him back into the club but we didn't have enough time.

"Go inside and get help," I told Ellie. "Call the police. Do both."

In what seemed like just a second later, Josh and I and our clothing rep buddies had our backs right up to the wall in front of Joyo's. There was nowhere to go but down the alley and I realized that was their plan. We'd likely find another group waiting at the next corner. No, it was better for us to take our chances here, where at least there were lights and other people.

It's been my experience that Aussies love a good bar fight. Ellie must have thought the same way because once back in the club, she headed straight for their table with the news that we were being mugged in the street. The Aussies came out of Joyo's in what looked like a rugby scrum formation and met the approaching group in the middle of the street. Man-on-man throw-downs commenced immediately.

My small group started mixing it up with the locals who had approached from the sidewalk. Traffic had stopped in the street going in both directions and the cars' headlights brightly illuminated the mayhem. I could hear police sirens. The two reps and I were taking some serious punches as we tried to stay around Josh. The Aussies made short work of their street fight and began pulling off our attackers. They really seemed to be having fun. The sirens were loud now and the locals started jumping back on their motorcycles to make a quick exit.

On cue, our Aussie rescuers launched into one of their drinking/kick-ass victory songs. They seemed to think that Josh and I had intentionally picked a fight with a bunch of locals, which made us hero warriors in their eyes. In reality, I had just been covering up, protecting Josh and trying to stay in one piece. For the rest of the trip it was impossible for me to go anywhere without being called "the mad fighting Yank" who had "single-handedly tried to take on all of Kuta Beach."

We all played dumb to the police, which came pretty easily. They could tell they weren't going to get anywhere with us. I'm sure that trying to deal with a large boisterous group of Aussies was one of the main reasons the police decided to tell everyone to leave the area. They knew the group was a bunch of surfers set to be in the big upcoming contest so they ordered us back to the hotel. Steve Reynolds and his merry band sang the entire way back to the Melasti.

* * * * *

Ellie and I were both too keyed up to go to sleep so we spread out on the couch in her room. Even though it was going to be rough, I was already thinking about surfing Ulu when the sun came up in a couple of hours. I called down to the front desk for breakfast and a pot of coffee. We laughed about the rough time Josh and a few of other hung-over surfers would have on the boats headed for G-

Land. The ride across the channel would wreak havoc with their queasy stomachs.

I wasn't sure how things would play out for me in the next few days so I just told Ellie that I would meet up with her and the team at G-Land as soon as I could. My priority was to track down any information I could get on Betet and that meant, at minimum, a trip to the PAB temple at Ubud.

When I left to grab my board from my room, Ellie was making her wake-up calls to organize the team's departure. I didn't envy her task.

Chapter 9

LOOKING FOR BETET

When I arrived at the reef, the tide was low and the sun was still rising. Scattered clouds were tinged with red and orange. I slowly walked out along the reef to a point deep enough to start paddling. The air temperature felt about 75, the water had to be 80 degrees and clean four-to-five foot swells were wrapping in, hitting the reef, jacking up and then peeling down the beach. What a beautiful morning.

I can't say I was the first one in the water but I was one of the few surfers out and I caught wave after wave for the first hour. But Bali is a destination point for people from around the world — especially from May through October when conditions are optimum for surfing and soon the lineup started to look like a meeting of the United Nations with locals, Aussies, Americans, Japanese, and citizens of virtually every European country paddling out.

So I did what I always do, I paddled down the beach where there were some big shifting peaks that no one was riding. No one was taking these waves because there was no real lineup. I just had to paddle to where my instincts directed me and then wait to get lucky. The take-off area was limited. I had to be in the right spot when a wave came in, practically right under the lip as it pitched over. Even a little way out of the impact zone and the wave was too mushy to paddle into. I don't mind this type of surfing because it means I can avoid the crowds that are centered in the generally accepted take-off area.

I started to pick up some waves once I figured out that I could take off virtually in the whitewater of the big peaks because they'd back off for a short period of time before jacking up on the inside reef, giving me time to get up and be ready for the oncoming section. After awhile, a couple of Aussies paddled into the same area and we shared waves but it never did get crowded. The tide continued to get higher and it hurt the waves, making them less frequent and less critical so after a good four-hour session, I decided to go in.

The entry to the reef at Ulu is through a beach cave that's shaped like a big funnel with high rocky walls on both sides. As the tide gets higher, the sandy beach disappears until just a small patch of sand is left at the end of the funnel where the steps up the bluff are located. The tide was at its maximum as I approached the beach cave and I realized I was being swept completely past and down the beach. I had forgotten that the current near the cave is so strong that if you miss the entrance your only recourse is to paddle all the way back out to the lineup and start over. I made it in on the second go-round and had to laugh at myself for making such a rookie mistake.

Back at the bungalows, Steve Roper was sitting in the patio area entertaining a Frenchman who was loudly complaining about how he had been run over and hit in the leg while surfing that morning. Steve looked at me and smiled, which I interpreted as an acknowledgment that the guy probably deserved it. But Steve is a gracious host so he managed to smooth the Frenchman's ruffled feathers — and probably earned a big tip to boot. Steve knew that I was in town with the White Sand team so he was surprised when I told him I was headed to the PAB temple in Ubud.

"The Brotherhood has become something of a problem here recently," he said. "I guess members have been harassing tourists at the airport. The cops have started picking them up. You can't mess with the tourism industry here. But in general, the PAB is mellow."

Steve confirmed that there were two PAB temples in Bali, the main one in Ubud and another smaller one along the coast road near Medewi.

Word on the melee at Joyo's had traveled fast and Steve wanted all the details. After I gave him the quick version, I went into the history of the situation that hadbrought me to Bali. I figured there was no reason why Steve shouldn't know what was going on.

The girls at the front desk called Wayan in cab #261 to pick me up. I could feel my battery starting to wear down but I figured I still had a couple of good hours left in me. Steve walked me to the cab and negotiated a fair price for the trip.

Ubud is not a long drive from Uluwatu but there's a lot of traffic so progress is slow. Traveling in a foreign country is never dull if you can gaze out the window and into other peoples' way of life. During the first part of our drive, we passed rows upon rows of shops and stores. Bali is like any other city; commercial and industrial activities are located in the population centers. Once traffic started to thin out so did the buildings and I enjoyed the view of open space and greenery just before we reached Ubud, which Wayan described as a Balinese cultural center.

The little town is a pleasant mix of art galleries, craft shops, restaurants, bars, hotels, and temples of every sort. The majority of Balinese are Hindu but Muslims, Buddhists and Christians are scattered throughout the island. There are also older supernatural beliefs that pervade the population, giving rise to small shrines everywhere that are adorned with cloth and parasols and filled with offerings of flowers, fruits and palm leaves. The Brotherhood has been active in the area for the last 40 years and its main temple fits right in against Ubud's diverse religious backdrop.

Wayan pulled over several times to ask for directions to the temple and we were eventually led to Monkey Forest Road. Wayan's English is fairly good so I had no trouble explaining the purpose of my trip. I showed him my picture of Betet and he agreed to accompany me into the temple as a translator. I carefully explained that the best way to get the information I was after was to say that I was a friend of Betet and that I was trying to locate him while on vacation in Bali. We pulled up to the entrance of a courtyard that fronted a large traditional style Balinese pavilion; its high four-sided roof supported by evenly-spaced pillars. There were a few people in the courtyard area but the scene was very quiet and I felt a little intimidated. This compound was much different from the one in Sycamore Grove.

We asked the first person we saw to tell us where we could inquire about a past member of the temple. We were sent around to the right of the main pavilion entry doors, where a series of offices lined the corridor. The second door we found was open and Wayan said the sign indicated it was an office. There wasn't anyone inside so we proceeded down the corridor and found a monk at work in another office.

Wayan inquired about membership information and the monk led us back to the original office, invited us to be seated and told us to wait.

After a couple of minutes, a trim little Balinese gentleman wearing a suit and tie came in and introduced himself in perfect English as Mr. Batur, the temple business manager. Mr. Batur listened to my question and explanation politely, looked at the picture and informed me that he had never seen Betet on the temple grounds in his nine years as business manager and would be very much surprised if Betet was a PAB member.

"Mr. Batur, I have come a long way to try and find my friend, Dede Betet. Could you do me a huge favor and check your office records? Maybe Dede was a member that you didn't know about."

"In a temple such as ours it would not be possible for me not to know a member but I will go to the other office and research his name if it will make you feel better. Please wait."

I felt like the proverbial dog who was being thrown a bone but I merely smiled and expressed my appreciation. When Batur returned he was shaking his head slowly from side to side as he took a seat behind the desk.

"It is as I said, Mr. Malone. No record of a Dede Betet. You must have gotten your information confused."

This was getting downright discouraging. Was it better to be persistent or go quietly? Either Batur was on the level or the fix was in but one more question probably was not going to make any difference.

"What about your other compound in Medewi; any chance he might have been a member there?"

"Impossible. Both compounds are linked and as I said, his name does not appear in our records. Medewi is very small, just a handful of devout monks who spend most of their time in meditation."

"So if I was to drive out there it would be a waste of time?"

"Complete waste of time I'm afraid. They do not allow visitors from the outside, it is a sacred sanctuary for the enlightened only."

We thanked Mr. Batur for his help and he politely gestured toward the door, although a little too quickly for my taste. Wayan and I hung around the courtyard area for awhile and passed out some copies of Betet's picture but each person gave us the same negative response. It appeared we had run into a dead end.

During the ride back, I mulled over my next step. By the time I returned to Uluwatu, I knew that a trip to the Medewi PAB compound was going to be necessary. Batur's comments about no visitors weren't going to stop me. I had come too far to overlook any possible chance of obtaining the information I was seeking.

I updated Steve and he called the G-Land satellite office in downtown Kuta and because he knew the office people and speaks the language, he was able to arrange for me to be driven to G-Land, allowing me to stop in Medewi along the way. Palms were greased and fees were paid. Almost everyone takes a boat from Kuta Beach to G-Land because it's much faster than the circuitous driving route but in travel terms Medewi is halfway to G-Land so it only made sense to continue the rest of the way by car.

Back at the bungalows, Steve and I sat in the cool dining area and he showed me how to operate his computer so I could e-mail Paul Maguire. I wanted to know if he had obtained any information from Harvey Patel regarding Betet. I logged into my account and started typing.

"Greetings from Indo. Anything from Patel regarding Betet?"

Paul replied almost immediately.

"He is not returning my calls. How are things going on your end?"

"Nothing doing at the Ubud temple. I will be going to the other temple tomorrow. Time to take off the kid gloves with Patel. At the very least he should be told what his guy Betet was up to. Besides, since Betet lived at the compound there are not likely to be any other sources of information about him."

"Understood, I will do my best. Take care."

116

I felt like I had just unleashed the dogs of war on Patel because I knew just how aggressive Paul could get but that's what happens when you don't return phone calls.

Dinner that night consisted of fish, rice and an assortment of fresh fruit eaten in the good company of the hotel's several European guests. Toward the end of the meal, my eyes were drooping and I began doing the head-bob thing. I was just able to make it to my room before I went comatose for the night.

Thankfully, my internal clock had adjusted to the local time so I woke up at sunrise. I pulled on my trunks, grabbed my board and headed to the beach. My surf session was very much like the one the day before. I surfed the inside section until it became too crowded then moved out to the shifty peak area where I did okay since I had a somewhat better understanding of the break.

I cut my surfing a little short to leave some time for packing before the driver came to pick me up. When I paddled in, I even managed to hit the beach cave entrance on my first try. As I neared the cave entrance, I spied a young surfer sitting on a small patch of sand on the side of the bluff. He had obviously missed the cave entrance and was trying to figure out what to do. I tried to signal with a hand motion to go around again but I was pushed into the cave before I could see that he understood. There's a lifeguard of sorts at Ulu but he's stationed up on top of the cliff, which isn't a very effective system because surfers on the beach can't see him, let alone hear him blowing his whistle.

Around the bungalows things were looking very much like a typical Balinese morning. A few people were eating breakfast, some were lounging poolside and the unhurried staff was serving breakfast and doing yard work. Yeah, I could get used to this.

I used the gardener's hose for my shower and then started moving my possessions down to the office. Steve was off somewhere but he had printed out an e-mail reply from Paul. He said Patel hadn't been very helpful. He merely agreed that he'd heard Betet had relatives in Indonesia but he said he had no further details and claimed to have no real personal knowledge of the man. The office ladies brought me some breakfast and coffee, which, together with a good night's sleep and satisfactory morning surf, put me in the right frame of mind to continue my journey.

The car was late so the ladies called the G-Land office and soon afterward the driver arrived. His name was Rizal and, unlike the local cabbie who wore a uniform, he was dressed casually in a T-shirt and shorts. I hadn't exchanged my dollars into Rupiahs so it took a group effort — including Rizal, who speaks English — to finally figure out my hotel bill. In the end, I threw in a $50 tip for the staff and everybody was happy.

Chapter 10

THE ROAD TO G-LAND

Rizal drives a big Isuzu van that has seen some hard miles. It squeaked and groaned but still had some pep and we motored right along. When I first attempted to fasten my seat belt, I discovered it had no buckles so the only alternative was to tie it across my chest. Next came the realization that that van had neither a working radio nor air conditioner, which didn't bother me that much because I've never owned a car with air conditioning. I joked about the van's deficiencies, saying that the company was showing Rizal no respect and that he should strike for better working conditions.

Rizal said he had transported many famous surfers to the surfing camp at G-Land and I encouraged him to tell me all about it. Listening to his stories helped to pass the time. He also told me about his job, wife and family and tried to explain to me the roadside scenes.

When we left the outskirts of the city, Bali transformed into a shimmering green landscape of palm trees and rice fields. Occasionally, we stopped at roadside warungs for local snacks but it was to be a long drive so we got back on the road quickly.

"So, why are you going to Medewi?"

I told Rizal I was stopping at the seaside village to search for my missing friend, Dede Betet, who had been a member of the PAB. Rizal was eager to volunteer information about Medewi since he drove by it almost weekly. He said he was from a village that was very similar to Medewi and explained that most Balinese villages are

119

usually laid out the same way with the temple, an open market area and the houses of the local nobility all set around a central area containing a large pavilion for community activities. Other private house compounds are usually laid out in rows surrounding the central area north-to-south or east-to-west with an additional temple at each end of the village. "But Medewi's layout is different because the PAB temple and compound are on the edge of the village."

Rizal said monks and initiates live at the compound and grow their own food in the neighboring fields. "And there's a commune near Medewi that's got close ties to the PAB. It's been around almost as long as the temple."

From Rizal's description, it sounded like the commune had grown, more or less, as an appendage of the PAB. He said people of all nationalities live in the commune and that they're all interested in the PAB or related to its members but don't necessarily want to live within the Brotherhood's compound. According to Rizal, the compound and the commune and all of their inhabitants are considered to be part of Medewi.

We were driving on a narrow two-lane road but it was paved so we were making good time. After several hours inland, the road began to wind back through the flat green rich fields towards the coast. We passed through a small village and the ocean came into view, sparkling blue in the bright afternoon sun. After a series of small coastal settlements, we reached Medewi. The village is near the main road so we parked close to a roadside warung that was doing a good business catering to passersby.

Rizal greeted his acquaintances at the warung and then motioned for me to follow him. The PAB temple was a short distance down the road, surrounded by a dense growth of trees and ferns. The temple's design is similar to the one in Ubud but this compound seemed to me to have a more serene vibe. Paths connect several structures and I could see people strolling between buildings. This was certainly nothing like the impression of the compound Mr. Batur gave me; there were no high walls or security gates.

Rizal stopped a man who was walking along the path and asked for information. The man seemed reluctant but gestured for us to wait and then he walked quickly towards the rear of the compound. A group of three monks — two Indonesians and a European — returned to where we were waiting. One of the Indonesian monks began talking to Rizal, who made his reply and then turned to me with the translation.

"The monks apologize for making us wait but they were not expecting visitors. They want to be of service but it's against policy to give out information on members."

"Tell them that Mr. Batur from Ubud sent me and that I've come a long way and I'm only trying to get information on a friend with whom I've lost contact over the years."

The mention of Batur's name got all three men's attention. I did feel a little guilty lying about Batur, and I was taking a chance that they would call for verification but I had come too far to be stopped now.

Rizal's translation to the monks seemed to go for a long time and involved a great deal of back-and-forth banter accompanied by hand gestures. He must have succeeded with his persuasive arguments because he took the Betet picture from me and handed it to the European monk who glanced at the picture and then handed it to one of the Indonesian monks. I thought I detected in the European's expression something like surprise at recognizing someone but soon the monks were shaking their heads and trying to return the picture as if it was burning their fingers.

"Rizal, ask them if they will do a record search to make sure there are no records of Betet's name."

At this point, all three began talking at one time, backing away, and shaking their heads.

Rizal replied. "They are insisting we leave before they are forced to call the authorities. They say they have answered our questions and can do nothing more to help."

I took the picture, which had Betet's face circled, and approached the European again. He shook his head vigorously and backed away. I showed the picture around one more time but I knew no one was going to admit recognizing Betet so we thanked them politely and left.

I was disappointed. I felt that at least one monk had recognized Betet but in the end I'd come up empty. I had the definite impression that the word was out not to talk to the "surfer from California."

There were quite a few people walking along the road to the village and the crowd at the roadside warung was still going strong when we returned to the van. I wasn't yet ready to admit defeat so I asked Rizal to accompany me to the village. It was market day in Medewi and there were numerous stalls set up in a very similar fashion to farmers' markets in the US. The locals and a few tourists were bargaining for fresh fruit and vegetables as well as a wide variety of handicrafts, woodcarvings, pottery, brightly-colored cloth, fans, parasols and all kinds of shells and jewelry. Near the edge of the market an older guy was playing a gamelan, which Rizal described as a local musical instrument comparable to a xylophone. The music was festive and an assemblage of children was romping around in rhythm to the tunes. There were kids ranging in age from toddler to teen. Some had very dark complexions while others were almost fair-skinned, which I took as indicative of the diversity in the village Rizal had mentioned.

I started showing my picture of Betet around. No one seemed to mind being bothered. Some of the kids even joined in to make a loud game of it, leading me from one villager to the next. One stall operator looked at the picture longer than the others and then apparently directed the children to take me to the pavilion located across from the market area. As we approached, most of the children stayed behind and only the two eldest children remained as my escorts. Sitting on mats in the pavilion was a group of traditionally-dressed and distinguished-looking gentlemen, whom I took to be the village elders.

Rizal approached them solemnly and addressed the elder seated in the middle of the group as "bapak," which means "father" and is a greeting of respect. Rizal continued speaking but I noticed he was asked no questions. The village elders seemed to be relaxed and they gestured at me to come closer. I handed my picture to the elder Rizal had addressed, who studied it for a time, and then he passed it to his neighbor. After the entire group had a good look, they wanted to know why I was interested in the man in the picture and they also wanted to know where the picture came from. The explanations took quite a while as all the elders took part in the conversation. Finally, Rizal turned to me.

"They have recognized the man as Dede Betet but also this man in the middle as Harvey Patel."

We were then invited to sit and the story was told, between puffs of locally grown tobacco, of how both Harvey Patel and Dede Betet had grown up in the sleepy seaside village of Medewi.

The elders said that about 30 years ago a young French woman had arrived at the commune. She'd been backpacking around Asia and had become interested in the PAB teachings. She settled in and eventually married Harvey Patel's father, who at that time was a monk studying at the compound. Their son grew up in and around the village and became very involved with the PAB as he grew older.

Dede Betet was a local boy who was friends with Harvey and shared his interest in the PAB. The two were companions and playmates all through their early years in the village.

Harvey's mother died when he was in his teens so he moved into the temple compound. He was apparently very bright and quickly became the temple's administrator and he appointed his friend Dede as his assistant.

Both young men were sent to Jakarta for their college educations and they did not return to their village. Harvey's father and Dede's parents passed away and neither Harvey nor Dede had been seen or heard from in many years.

I was still trying to process that the two had grown up together when Rizal turned to me. "One of the elders wants to know why Harvey's older half-brother, Sammy, is not in the picture."

I knew nothing about any half-brother so I asked Rizal to find out what he could.

"Apparently, Harvey's mom had originally arrived in the village with her young son, Sammy."

As the boys grew up, the elders said, Sammy was always in the company of Harvey and Dede. It was a rare thing to see one without the other two although Sammy's European looks did set him apart from his buddies. Sammy left the village around the same time as Harvey and Dede. The elders were unsure of his destination but they knew he was not college bound.

"Ask them if they know Sammy's last name."

"They say his last name is Patel. They also say that while Sammy was a PAB member he wasn't as into it as much as Harvey and Dede. He spent much of his time at the beach. He was one of the first village kids to be talented at surfing and he liked hanging out with surfers whenever they visited the village."

At this point, Rizal asked a question and the group talked for a couple more minutes.

"I asked them to explain why they call Sammy 'lelipi cerik,' which means 'little snake.' They say that one day Sammy had to be carried back from the beach by a group of surfers. He had landed on the reef and had a deep gash on the back of his shoulder. The monks at the compound gave him medical attention and he recovered fine but he was left with an elongated "s"-shaped scar. That's how he got the nickname 'little snake.'"

I couldn't think of any other questions so Rizal and I stood up to leave. We thanked the elders for their kindness and told them that their information would most certainly help me to locate my missing friend. We wandered around the market place for a bit longer and I made several purchases, things that I really didn't need but I felt like it was good way to thank the entire village for their hospitality and the information I received.

At last I had some concrete background and facts. Betet may have given the instructions regarding Bobby's attack — and who knows what else — but Harvey Patel was most certainly involved, if not the real leader. It was looking like two high-ranking, lifelong members of the PAB gave the orders but I was still left with the question of motive. What did the Brotherhood have to gain by taking out one, possibly two, world-class surfers? I didn't know of any connections between the Brotherhood and the top-ranked surfers but facts don't lie and the facts were saying that the Brotherhood was responsible. I had to just keep digging and see what turned up.

* * * * *

When we got back on the road, I tried a cell phone call to Paul Maguire but I couldn't get a signal so there was nothing I could do but sit back and enjoy the ride. I felt good that my trip was taking me across half of Bali and a portion of Java; it was an opportunity to see much more of the country than I would during a boat ride across the channel. After leaving Medewi, we traveled inland again and while taking in the scenery, I'd ask Rizal an English word and he would give the Indonesian translation, which I would write down phonetically. This helped to pass the time and Rizal seemed to enjoy my clumsy attempts to speak his language, which has a lyrical quality about it.

The countryside was lush and green, a series of undulating rice fields were broken up only by palm trees and interconnecting dirt roads and an occasional small village or roadside warung. We passed through a fairly large town and came back out on the coast road again at a place called Candi Kusuma. The road continued within sight of the Bali Strait, which is part of the Indian Ocean.

When we reached the ferry to Gilimanuk we were able to drive directly aboard, a feat that produced a big smile on Rizal's face. "That's a relief. It could be up to two hours wait for the next ferry."

The van ended up parked at the front of the ferry, near the off-loading ramp. The cars were so tightly packed, I could barely open the door to get out. Rizal immediately crawled into the back of the van and went to sleep while I, being a typical tourist, wanted to roam about and observe the hustle and bustle of the loading procedure. There were several other ferries making the crossing at the same time but ours was the biggest and it was laden with all types of vehicles and passengers. I watched our crossing, which took about an hour, from the upper observation deck.

Gilimanuk is a large coastal town that is similar to Kuta Beach, only without the tourists. Rizal negotiated a jumble of cars, pedestrians and the ever-present motorbikes buzzing in and out of traffic with only inches to spare. Once we reached the outskirts of town, the scenery began to take on a rural appearance. The paved road ended and I quickly found out why most people take the boat to G-Land. The dirt roads were in terrible shape with big potholes and long stretches of "wash boarded" areas that could only be driven at a maximum speed of 15 MPH. There should have been a road sign posted with the message "Guaranteed to rattle the fillings right out of your teeth."

Twilight found us on a long narrow section of "roadway" passing through a forest of trees with long, straight trunks. No one else was in sight and the atmosphere was eerie. A few hours later, the terrain changed to lush tropical forest, which grew to within inches of the road and seemed to threaten to engulf our van. Being surrounded by jungle was disorienting and I quickly lost track of time. Rizal told me we had entered the Banguwangi Selatan Nature Preserve. The area was so remote and the jungle so dense that I would not have been at all surprised if we'd come upon one of the preserve's famous Sumatran tigers. But thankfully, the dirt road conditions soon improved and we starting making better time; Rizal drove steadily onward in the pitch-blackness.

When the G-Land surf camp appeared in the headlights, Rizal announced that it was 11:00 p.m. He said it as if he'd just won a race. I said a tired good-bye to him and pressed a big bill into his hand. The last five hours of the drive were pretty brutal and I attempted to use some of my new Indonesian vocabulary to thank him for all his help. I literally could not have done it without him. He told me cheerily that he'd be on the road again early in the morning.

There was still some activity around the camp but the staff was not used to such late arrivals. The people surrounding the bar were shooting curious glances in my direction. Because I arrived alone by van, they thought I was some type of VIP or a personal friend of the camp's Indonesian owner.

My bungalow had been booked as part of the White Sand Surf Team contingent and I was happy to find a king-size bed with a canopy of mosquito netting. Best of all, there were no roommates. As soon as my boards were delivered, I fell into a deep sleep.

Chapter 11

G-LAND SURF CAMP

Over the course of surfing's history, traveling surfers seeking waves and adventure have discovered many ideal and isolated surf destinations. Inevitably, the surf camp phenomenon followed and so surf traveling is now more organized and far less adventurous. But I like to think there are still breaks waiting to be discovered.

There are three surf camps located along the one-mile long reef at Garajagan, known as G-Land. The oldest camp, Bobby's Camp, has been around at least 30 years and hosts the contest. When I awoke in the morning, I could hear the muted voices of people walking by my bungalow on their way to breakfast. Bobby's Camp is set up as a series of bungalows spread around a central open pavilion that serves as the dining and bar area. The Indonesian staff keeps the camp in tight working order and the grounds are well maintained; paths wind around the bungalows and through the property, cutting though the abundant natural jungle foliage.

Camp guests choose from three packages: "Standard" includes three bottles of beer per day, "Deluxe" offers five beers and "Superior" guarantees eight bottles of beer per day. All the packages also include three meals a day and various upgrades in rooms and bathroom facilities are available. The beer-per-day aspect is kind of a joke but after the bar tab is tallied up at the end of a trip, the final bill at a surf camp is often not so funny.

I knew the tide was low and therefore there was no real hurry for me to get in the water, but a surf check was still my first priority. We were all counting on a big swell arriving any day. This time of year in Bali and G-Land there are prevailing offshore winds that usually pick up around mid-morning. The winds greatly improve the shape of the waves, so many people sleep late in expectation of the offshore winds.

I'm usually not good for much in the morning until I have at least one cup of coffee so my plan was to make a quick and quiet stop at the pavilion to grab some caffeine and then hike down to the beachfront viewing area. The plan was solid except the dining room had been reorganized since my last trip so when I entered where I thought the self-serve coffee was set out, it turned out I'd walked right into the main dining area where a handful of Aussies were eating breakfast. I was immediately greeted loudly as the famous Kuta Beach brawler who had single-handedly taken on a swarm of howling local boys. I recognized all the guys as members of the rescue party so I figured they deserved to have their fun but when they started to do a ring announcer routine with me as the victorious fighter, I found my exit.

The path from the pavilion leads to a clearing near the water's edge that's used as a surf check spot. A few tables, a couple of hammocks and some chairs were scattered about the clearing. Several guys were already there scanning the horizon. There was definitely a swell running.

The waves at G-Land break a long way out from shore and, especially at low tide, it can be pretty tough to see what's really going on in the lineup. On my last trip, I discovered fun surf with only a few people in the water while everyone else was waiting for it to get good. As I walked the path back to camp, I met Ellie so I turned around and walked back down to the clearing with her. She was having a bad morning.

"Only three of Josh's boards made it here. We left the hotel with five."

Professional surfers usually travel from contest to contest with several different boards to make sure they have the correct board for the surfing conditions on any given day. Contest heats were already underway. For Josh, not having all his regular boards was a major handicap.

"We've searched the camp from top to bottom — nothing."

I knew, that as team manager, Ellie was feeling responsible for the missing boards but I assured her it wasn't her fault. "There's no way you could have physically watched every board during the trip here."

Josh's remaining personal boards were now being kept inside Ellie's bungalow and various other surf team members had already volunteered their boards, if necessary, for Josh's use. Ellie said some of her guys were in today's heat with an 11:00 a.m. start but Josh wasn't scheduled to surf until tomorrow so her assistant and a camp employee were in the process of doing another search for the lost boards. I offered to help her with the search but she said she had it covered.

I quickly filled her in on the discovery I made about the close connection between Harvey Patel and Dede Betet and its implications as far as who was responsible for Bobby's attack and Ramon's death. "I'm going to call Paul and bring him up to speed. Have you made calls yet? How's the reception?"

"Yeah, I've talked to Paul this morning. Reception comes and goes and you'll get some dropped calls but now is good time to try him since it's early evening back home."

I wished Ellie luck with the search and headed back to my bungalow to call Paul. He was intrigued, to say the least, by my new information.

"So they grew up side by side in the same village? Now, that's interesting, especially since Patel told me that Betet was just an office assistant hired by the Brotherhood's Central Administration Center who had only worked there a few months."

"So you finally got a chance to talk to Patel?"

"Yeah, I blindsided him on his way into a public hearing regarding his Leucadia project. He acted completely shocked when I told him about Betet's involvement with Bobby's attack, denied any involvement and promised a full internal investigation. Patel's got to be dirty. He had to have known what Betet was up to."

"I've given this a lot of thought and I think you're right. The only problem is we can't prove a thing. All Patel has to do is pull the old politician trick and deny, deny, deny. Given his position in the community he would be believed and we would look foolish."

"So we do nothing?"

"I hate to say it, Paul, but that seems like the best course of action. For right now, we let things play out and then see if down the road we can really use this info to our advantage. There is still the very slim chance that Patel is innocent in all this."

"Okay, so then it's no harm no foul and we don't end up looking like we're tripping over our own feet accusing innocent people. Seems like the smart play. As long as nobody else gets hurt."

"Remember Paul, we both had our suspicions about the involvement of one of the clothing companies and I'm not ready to throw that theory out the window. Maybe Betet was working by himself within the Brotherhood, but what was his motive? What was he trying to accomplish? As far as we know, any one of the clothing companies has a better motive than Betet."

"All right, so we're agreed. We do nothing for now, just sit back and watch. But hey, keep a close eye on Josh and do your best to make sure nobody else gets hurt. And try and have some fun. We'll talk again soon."

* * * * *

Now that I'd taken care of business, it was time to hit the surf.

I'm not a big experimenter when it comes to my surfing equipment; once I find something I like I stick with it. My boards are longer than the average short board but since it's a constant battle for me to keep my weight under 200 pounds, I've found I need the extra flotation. I have three favorite boards. My pineapple model by Bill Shrosbree is more of a fun shape, a 7'2" thruster with a thumbnail-shaped tail. My 7'6" thruster by Skip Frye is narrower and has a faster shape that I use in larger surf. The Frye works like magic in Bali. It has a slight V in the tail area that, combined with its fast drawn-out tail section design, allows the off-shore wind to flow under the board, causing a hydroplaning sensation at extremely high speeds.

Shrosbree and Frye have been shapers since the mid-1960s. Both are still going strong although I've heard rumors that Frye, who is somewhat of a legend now, is taking on less work. Shrosbree can usually be found in his shaping room in Encinitas and anyone who is willing to wait the necessary time can get one of his custom handmade boards. I'm riding my third "Shros" and I hope there will be a fourth and a fifth. Lately, at my home break in Encinitas, I've been testing out some promising new designs being produced by a homegrown shaper, Jeff "Rat" Battisti of Rat Surfboards.

During low tide at G-Land it's necessary to walk over the exposed reef for about a quarter of a mile until you get to a point where there is enough water to start paddling. Care and patience are crucial for those of us who don't wear protective reef walker booties. Once you're in the surf zone, the current flows down the reef at such a rate that you have to paddle constantly just to stay in one place. G-Land makes you work for every wave, but it's oh, so worth it. The best waves I've ever seen or ridden were at this fabled Indonesian surf spot. The waves are powerful, fast, and hollow and the rides are long. But if you get caught in the impact zone on a big day, you can expect to be treated very rudely.

As I paddled out, memories of my last trip to this famous reef came flooding back. I came down with a low-grade fever and stomach flu and, just to make things a little better, towards the end of the trip I managed to break a bone in my hand during a fall on a powerful top-to-bottom eight-foot wave. Yet, even with the flu I managed to surf every day and was also able to establish some lineups or take off areas that worked for me in and around the upper end of the reef.

There were only a few other surfers in the water and there were some waves coming through but there was not much water covering the reef so I had to select waves carefully. By my California standards, the waves were great and I had to keep reminding myself that I really was surfing the legendary spot featured so many times in magazines and movies.

After awhile, the professional surfers started paddling out, some as a warm-up for their upcoming heats, others just for a "free surf" session. Surfing with the pros is not a recommended activity for the recreational surfer; after all, these guys are among the best in the world. But competition for waves is part of the sport and, generally speaking, if you get yourself into the best position to catch a wave, that wave is usually yours to ride. I had already gotten more than a few good waves so I let myself just enjoy being in the water and I watched the pros shred the now six-foot peeling lefts. But soon enough, wave envy got the better of me and I decided to make a move. I paddled up the reef and stationed myself further in and over than everybody else. Two of the world's best surfers, who were sitting together waiting for a set, looked at me as if to say, "You have got to be kidding — you really think you're going to ace us out of a wave?" I only did it to mess with their minds. Plus, there was an outside chance of picking up a wave. I paid the price for my arrogance by getting caught inside by the next set of waves so the pros had the last laugh after all.

Competing for waves is just not my style. I surf for the enjoyment and the adrenaline rush and so that I can appreciate nature and escape the hassles and irritations of everyday life. I started drifting down the one-mile long reef. I always prefer to move to an area away from the crowds — there may be fewer waves but when a wave does come, you know it's yours. I spent another two hours drifting, paddling and picking up long hollow waves.

* * * * *

As I walked back up the beach towards camp, I could see the contest was in full swing. The swell was on the rise and all other conditions were favorable — the air temperature was 95 degrees and the water temperature was 85 degrees. Surf contests at these remote exotic locations are very much like the proverbial three-ring circus. Out in the water, boats of all shapes and sizes clustered near the break and water rescue workers on Jet Skis were at the ready. About 300 yards from shore, the contest judges were stationed on a bamboo scaffolding structure that the surf camp staff erected on the reef. There were many photographers and onlookers in the water but that was nothing compared to the crowd on the beach. Every inch of sand seemed to be spoken for with several temporary pavilions covered with sponsor banners claiming quite a bit of the real estate. All the big contests have a main sponsor. Because Indonesia is practically in Australia's backyard, this contest's sponsor is Steve Reynolds's Koala Clothing Company and its official name is the Koala G-Land Open.

The competition begins with a series of elimination heats, then four-man quarterfinals, followed by two-man semi-finals and a two-man final. The judges utilize a 10-point scoring system per wave and count the best two waves of each heat. The number of near 10-point waves was increasing with each heat, a clear sign that this contest was going to be an epic event.

It was early afternoon by the time I finished my surf and walked into the camp's bustling viewpoint. Looking seaward, I saw the long blue lines peeling down the reef as the offshore wind blew spray high into the air off the wave face. Surfers in brightly-colored contest T-shirts dropped down the wave faces only to disappear into gaping barrels. As I stood watching the contest, I heard two nearby spectators talking about drama in the elimination heats. Apparently, the Brazilians were pulling out all the stops to advance their surfer to the finals and some interferences, along with pushing and shoving, had occurred.

I headed back to my bungalow for a refreshing cold shower. A few minutes later, I was back at the beach, armed with my binoculars and a bottle of water. I found a seat on a two-story viewing stand. The view through my binoculars made me feel like I had a front row seat at the latest surf flick. The pros were shredding eight-to-10 footers. But the sets were coming less frequently as the tide filled in and just before dusk the contest was called for the day.

Dinner is one of the few times when everyone in camp is at the same place at the same time so the pavilion was packed. The seating arrangement broke down predominantly by country of origin. I managed to acquire a seat next to Ellie and we discussed the day's events while we ate.

"So how did Josh do in his heat today?" I asked.

"Josh pulled out a win, but he would have done better if he had his favorite board."

"Nothing new on the missing boards then?"

"Nope, vanished into thin air somewhere between here and Kuta Beach."

"How are your other team members doing?"

"They're doing all right, nothing too surprising. Mostly seconds and thirds. Man, the Brazilians are really playing dirty. They're pushing, they're shoving and they're back-paddling people. I've heard the contest organizers are going to make an announcement to try to put an end to it."

"Those kind of tactics and interference calls will only hurt them in the long run. Heard from our fearless leader?"

"I sent Paul an e-mail but I haven't heard back yet. I know it's driving him crazy that he can't get me on my cell phone whenever he wants."

"Well, it's such a close race this year. I think everybody is more than a little anxious." The Australian surfer, Sid Barrow, was currently slightly ahead in points but Josh, Pietro Pradratz, and Butch Chu were all still within striking distance. They all needed respectable finishes in this contest to stay in contention.

The dining hall was unusually subdued for a gathering of surfers. Each group was keeping more or less to itself. The interaction between the Brazilians and Hawaiians was blatantly tense and the Hawaiians' company owner, Sam Woods, was talking quietly to his guys. I noticed only a few of the people at his table were drinking alcohol and all were intently listening to his words.

Ellie asked if she could use my bungalow for a team meeting immediately after dinner so I gave her the key. Privacy in the crowded surf camp was a rare commodity. As dinner was being cleared, I walked over to check in with the Aussies and, as soon as they spotted me, they started in humming the theme song from "Rocky." (For the next few days, my new nickname was "Rocky.") The Australians were in high spirits, as usual. Sid had won his heat and it was bottles of the local brew Bintang all around. I congratulated Sid on his win and we started discussing how unbelievably good the waves were. If the swell continued and the surfers kept up their game, this contest could produce the most perfect 10-point waves ever.

The planned evening entertainment got underway — a gamelan percussion orchestra accompanied by graceful Balinese dancers. The atmosphere became relaxed and conversation flowed more freely but there was still an undercurrent of tension in the room. Ellie and her team members returned from their meeting.

"I heard back from Paul," she said as she handed me my key. "He thinks Josh's missing boards are part of a conspiracy. Apparently, he's now convinced that someone, or one of the clothing companies, is intent on dominating the industry."

A little later, I happened to be standing with a group that included Ellie and Josh when Pedro Valiz strolled over to congratulate Josh on his heat win. But he did it in such a way that his lack of sincerity was obvious. "Nice job out there Josh. You got lucky;, my guy was having an off day."

He addressed the group. "Paul told me what happened to Bobby and Arrington. He thinks somebody is trying to win the world title by eliminating the top guys. I think it's all just a big coincidence. Pietro is going to win it all this year."

Ellie went after him. "Really, Pedro? If Pietro is so good, why does your team need to resort to such underhanded tactics?"

Apparently, Valiz was not used to being questioned. His face turned red and he replied angrily, in Portuguese, before stomping away.

"What did he just say?" Josh asked.

Brazilian surfer Marcos Viene happened to be standing with our group. "Trust me," he said. "You don't want to know."

Valiz certainly wasn't doing the public image of his company much good. People were already talking about his team's antics in the water and now he'd cussed out a popular female surf team manager. A couple of media types were within earshot; I knew one worked for a major surf magazine.

The evening had been eventful but nothing could stop the yawns that began escaping from my mouth. I excused myself and followed the dimly lit path to my bungalow in the Javanese jungle.

* * * * *

I was up in the predawn darkness, ready to grab a few of those famous G-Land barrels before the contest crowd descended in force. The tide was very low but as the new day broke there was still a good strong swell coming down the reef. Nobody was in the water yet. Progress over the exposed reef was torturously slow but it gave me time to study the lineup and pick the best area to get into some good surf. The waves were much bigger and more powerful than they looked from the beach and seeing how shallow the reef was in the area called "launching pads" definitely led me to have some second thoughts before I committed to paddling into my first wave.

This particular wave was probably average size for the day but still well overhead. The only thing I had time to do was get to the bottom of the wave as it jacked-up on the reef, then I turned and pulled in tight as I rocketed down the line as fast as my Magic Frye could take me. The wave was incredibly long and hollow and I stayed locked in the entire time until at the very end when I pulled one cutback and then turned back up the wave face and glided out over the shoulder into the flat water.

When I looked up, I saw Josh paddling out. He flashed me a big smile and a shaka sign. While I waited for him, I saw a small swarm of surfers entering the water, all traveling slowly over the shallow reef. Today it was going to get crowded out here early.

Josh and I talked a little bit about his upcoming heat. He seemed confident of doing well but was still really missing his favorite board, which was among those that hadn't turned up. As it got more and more crowded, I managed to catch a few more waves but none was as good as that first down-the-line beauty. It seems that frequently the first wave of a session ends up being the best wave of the day.

After awhile, I just let myself drift down the reef to escape the crowds. I managed to pick up some nice long barrels and I thought about how the worst day at G-Land is better than 90 percent of the surf days in Southern California.

I often play mind games while surfing. Sometimes a word will just pop into my head and I'll repeat it over and over again or spell it in different ways. I do it with series of numbers too, combining them in different ways. I don't know why I play these mental games with myself. I'm not sure if other people do the same, but it just seems to occur spontaneously so I assume it is something my subconscious mind needs to do. Or maybe it just helps me concentrate. On this particular morning, while surfing at a far-off exotic beach, the word that was running through my mind like a mantra, being repeated over and over again was "Wednesday." The odd spelling of the word, as opposed to the way it's pronounced, has always intrigued me. Today is Saturday. Go figure.

As I walked back up the beach toward camp, I scanned the sand for tiger tracks. As the story goes, some of the first surfers to discover this spot found tiger tracks on the beach one morning so they immediately began construction of a tree house that would allow them to sleep safely at night.

While surfing, I had drifted almost the entire length of the reef but I still arrived at camp in time to listen in on the pre-contest meeting. Almost everyone in camp was gathered in the pavilion area. The quarter-final heats were scheduled to start at 11:00 a.m. One of the Aussie organizers picked up a megaphone and outlined the day's program in loud bursts. He signed off with a warning that "no further unsportsmanlike conduct of any sort will be tolerated and the offending person will be immediately ejected." An awkward moment followed, as it seemed that every person present turned and looked at the Brazilian contingent, whose members glared back at the crowd.

The heat sheet for the day had already been posted:

Chu (Hawaii) vs. Parker (Australia)
Smith (USA) vs. Pradratz (Brazil)
Barrow (Australia) vs. Garcia (Hawaii)
Phillips (USA) vs. Rizo (Brazil)

Down at the beach, Ellie and her team members, along with many other people, were preparing to board a large spectator boat that has a shallow draft well suited for anchoring near the line up. They'd have a front row view of the contest. I decided to stay on the beach. The binoculars worked really well from the viewing stand and I could still paddle out for a closer look later in the day.

As I walked back to the pavilion to grab some breakfast, I greeted some of the local staff working on the grounds. Indonesians usually greet each other whether or not they are acquainted. It creates a friendly atmosphere. Besides, I wanted a chance to practice my limited vocabulary.

I was finishing up my meal when Sam Woods, owner of Hawaii's Third Reef Clothing Company, walked up with his tray of food and took a seat across from me. I quickly decided to use my stock Indonesian greeting on him.

"Ken ken bli bagus." I said.

He just looked at me blankly and shook his head, indicating he did not understand. This conversation was off to a real good start. We began talking generally about the contest and how the close race for number one had evolved. His Hawaiians were performing very well, steadily advancing through the heats in a workmanlike manner.

Sam Woods is something of an enigma in the surfing community. He didn't grow up at the local beaches of Hawaii. He just kind of appeared on the scene and single-handedly started up a small clothing company that became one of the biggest and most dynamic in the industry. I've heard that Sam has a low-key style about him. He stays in the background while offering encouragement to his surfers and helping out with the details of managing the team.

"Has there been any progress on figuring out who attacked Bobby?"

His question surprised me since I'm not officially part of the White Sand Surf Team. I decided to play dumb, which is usually the best idea — say as little as possible and listen carefully. "Not as far as I know. It's still pretty much a mystery who is responsible."

"Yeah, Paul Maguire called to warn me to watch my team members. He thinks it's possible there may be more attacks. I hope that's not the case. And I hope they catch whoever hurt Bobby and put them away for a long, long time."

"I think it's just a matter of time before they catch the guy, Sam. You can't attack a famous world class surfer and expect to get away with it."

I thought he looked a little surprised by my comment. "Right, of course."

He changed the subject. "What about those Brazilians?" he said with a laugh. "They're pulling out all the stops. Old Pedro really wants to win it. Even after that warning this morning, I doubt they can finish up the contest without any more problems. They've been nothing but trouble all year."

"Yeah, that's what Ellie's been telling me. Too bad they just can't be mellow and play by the rules."

"Well, Mike, I guess some people like to make up their own rules."

I was sitting with an empty tray in front of me so it seemed like a good time to make an exit. "I'll see you later, Sam. Good luck out there today."

I headed for the viewing stand and on the way, I thought about the Brazilians. So far, their group certainly seemed like the most likely to play dirty and if winning was that important to them maybe they were responsible for what happened to Bobby and Ramon and Arrington as well. But was there a connection between the Brazilians and the PAB? I decided to stop trying to put the pieces of the puzzle together because, to borrow a line from a TV character, I had insufficient information and things did not compute.

By the time I focused on the surf, the first 30-minute heat was already in progress. The waves were nearly perfect eight-to-10-foot barrels and the pros were loving it. The conditions were so fast that there was not a lot of time for maneuvers other than a few snapbacks under the lip and the occasional floater. The contest was coming down to who could make the takeoff, get the farthest back in the tube for the longest period of time and still make the wave.

For me, surfing is about pushing the limits of a person's ability; it's not enough just to make the wave. But there's a fine balance that needs to be maintained between attempting radical maneuvers and successfully riding the wave to its completion. If I see a surfer try a maneuver without a chance of completing it then, to me, he has just wasted a wave, which goes against a basic tenet of surfing: Waves are made to be ridden not wasted. That said, I think it's worse to play it safe, do nothing and make the wave than it is to try something radical and fall off.

In any sport, there must be people out in front leading the way and pushing the limits. Surfers' willingness to try new maneuvers keeps the sport evolving and consequently leads to breakthroughs in materials and design. The aerials, 360s, reverses, flips, tail slides and other moves now being performed by young surfers are truly amazing, especially when they're successfully used to get the most out of a wave. There's a lot of conversation between proponents of the so-called "old school" of rail-to-rail power surfing and the progressive "new school" of aerials and so-called tricks. It's not a question of which is better — there's a time and a place for both (sometimes on the same wave). One thing for certain is that there is currently a strong youth movement of above-the-lip surfing that is here to stay. It's up to the individual surfer, according to his ability, to push his own boundaries. And when a good surfer with natural ability is in his prime, there is practically no limit to what can be accomplished on a wave. Where the mind goes, the body can follow.

Heats one and two were completed and I intended to paddle out to the lineup for the final two heats to get a closer view. Watching from the water is a beautiful experience, better than the best surf movie. Sid and his Hawaiian opponent were going barrel-to-barrel and I did not envy the judges' task. Sid seemed to have a slight edge because of his wave selection and he managed to stay back in the tube a little longer. In the end, Sid was declared the winner.

The final heat of the day was Josh versus the Brazilian, Rizo. Both were already in the water waiting for the start of the heat and with the approach of a nice-looking set, the starter horn sounded. Josh is a goofy-foot, which means he surfs facing the wave. This gave him a slight advantage over Rizo, who's a regular foot and surfs with his back to the wave.

Josh had inside position and decided to go on the second wave of the set. He surfed it perfectly, managing a stand-up barrel on the outside followed by a pull in cover up through the speed section. It had to be a 10-point wave.

Rizo dropped in on the last wave of the set and surfed fairly well, pulling off a couple of near-vertical snapbacks before a good cover up on the inside.

The tide was starting to get a little too high, causing the set waves to come less frequently and both surfers were forced to wait out a 10-minute lull before the next waves arrived. Josh again had inside position and priority so Rizo got overeager and took off on the first wave while Josh paddled and waited.

Rizo's wave was okay but definitely below par for what was available. Josh got into an eight-foot bomb that he handled really well, although he did seem a little tentative on his cutbacks. It appeared that his board was just a little too loose for the conditions.

There was no doubt that Josh had already won the heat. Rizo wouldn't be able to catch up now unless Josh failed to catch another wave, which was not going to happen. Josh was already paddling for another outside feathering beast. He made a nice bottom turn, waiting ever so slightly for the next section to develop, then he pulled in and disappeared inside the barrel.

Rizo, assuming that Josh was not going to make the wave, turned at the last possible second and took off on a vertical face. His board released at the top of the wave and he free fell, landing squarely on top of Josh who had just miraculously emerged from the wave.

Immediately, the Jet Ski rescue teams deployed. Neither surfer looked to be in very good condition. Both floundered in the whitewater trying to recover their boards — Josh's was in two pieces.

Rizo's head was bleeding. I started to paddle over to see if I could be of any help but the guys were already being loading onto the Jet Ski sleds for the trip back to the spectator boat, where the medical team was waiting.

By the time the Jet Skis were headed back to the boat, everyone had recovered their senses and the screaming and finger-pointing began in earnest in about six different languages. Nobody could understand what anybody else was saying.

I paddled to the boat to try to get some news. Josh had gotten on the Jet Ski sled under his own power but I still wanted to hear firsthand that he was okay. The scene on the boat was chaotic with the multilingual shouting match in full swing so I sat by as they powered up the boat and headed for the channel.

The heat was called and Josh was declared the winner. Rizo was disqualified. Josh, Sid, Chu, and Pradratz were headed to the semis.

There was nothing for me to do so I started paddling over to the take off area as fast as I could. The lineup was filling up quickly and I realized that even one wave to myself under these circumstances was unlikely. I stayed out just long enough to get picked off by a cleanup set — probably the last major set of the day before the tide got too high. My surf leash broke so I had to swim all the way to the lagoon to retrieve my board.

When I finally reached my board, I saw other boards floating nearby. It made me feel better to know that I wasn't the only person who had been snuffed by the sneaker set.

As I walked down to the channel where the off-loading from the spectator boat was happening, I kept getting bits and pieces of information. Josh was okay. He had a bruise and soreness in his calf muscle. The White Sand team was arriving on the beach when I got to the landing area. Josh was upright and walking but he was favoring his left leg. I congratulated him on his win and told him he was lucky that all he got out of the deal was a bruised leg.

Rizo was still aboard the boat, receiving medical attention. I prepared myself for the emotions at the camp. I knew many people believed Rizo had intentionally dropped in on Josh. Nobody on the beach seemed to know the best way to treat Josh so Ellie decided he should be driven back to camp where the on-call doctor could be consulted.

A while later, Ellie and I were sitting on my front porch, Bintangs in hand and ready to make a scheduled phone call to Paul Maguire. Paul had watched the live webcast of the contest so he already knew Josh had won the heat but he immediately asked about the extent of his

Josh's injuries. Ellie did her best to reassure Paul that Josh was okay and following doctor's orders but she also warned him that nobody could be sure how Josh's injured calf muscle was going to feel by tomorrow's semi-final heat.

Ellie inquired about the status of the new boards that had already been ordered for Josh — he would need a whole new quiver for the Hawaiian contest — and then handed the phone to me.

"You've been getting some of that good surf, Mike? It's been total crap here."

"Yeah, the surf has been epic. I've managed to get in some sessions. Everything's good on this end, no developments to report in our ongoing mystery. But I'm more than a little worried about what's going to happen once we get to Hawaii. This camp is pretty safe but Hawaii is a whole new ball game and I'm going to need some help. How about Wayne flies out with Josh's new boards? That way we know the boards will get there and I know I've got my back up. I already talked to Wayne about the possibility of him coming over and he's ready to go when needed."

"You read my mind, Mike. I'll give Wayne a call and get things organized. I'll get there before the contest starts and I'm going to bring Bobby with me if his doctors give him the okay."

After I hung up with Paul, I persuaded Ellie to stick around for a second beer. Since our arrival at G-Land, things had cooled off quite a bit between us. The problems with Josh and the pressure of the contest had caused her to adopt an all-business attitude, which was perfectly understandable but I know that isn't her true personality and I felt like she deserved a bit of a break. We both put our feet up on the deck railing and greeted other guests as they walked by. Darkness settled into camp.

A little while later, as I made my way to dinner along the dimly lit pathway, I passed two men speaking rapid-fire

Indonesian. I recognized one as the camp manager but the other man had his back to me so it was not until I moved to walk around them that I recognized him as Sam Woods. Neither of them seemed to notice when I muttered my Indonesian greeting. I was thinking to myself that Woods had indicated to me during breakfast the other day that he didn't understand Indonesian when I heard loud cheering coming from the pavilion so I continued on my way. Turned out the Aussies were toasting Sid Barrow. What a surprise.

This evening was likely the last that everyone would be at camp so the staff pulled out all the stops for dinner and entertainment. A gamelan orchestra provided Balinese music while male and female performers entertained us with traditional dances. Indonesians are a gracious, hospitable and welcoming people. Much of their music and dance has religious origins but they've adapted to entertaining tourists — the music was loud and percussive and the costumes bright and exotic.

A number of local officials, some in suit and tie, others in traditional ceremonial dress, were in attendance. They started off the evening with several short speeches that consisted mainly of the Indonesian hosts welcoming the professional surfers and then our group thanking our Indonesian hosts. It all felt very genuine but I have to say the best part of the evening was the food: traditional dishes of grilled meats and fish for the carnivores as well as rice and vegetable dishes and fruit platters for the many surfers following a vegetarian or vegan diet.

As soon as dinner was cleared, the local dignitaries said their goodbyes. The staff rearranged the tables and the surfing community was left to its own devices, which is just they way they like it. One of the main topics of conversation all night had been whether Rizo dropped in on Josh accidentally or if it had been intentional. Feelings were running high on both sides of the debate and fueled by the large quantities of the potent local alcohol called Arak that many in the crowd had enjoyed during dinner.

The semi-final match-ups were posted and people took turns gathering around the board to have a look and weigh in on their favorites. The final would take place directly after the semis, which would start at 11:00 a.m. When Josh walked into the pavilion with his teammates before dinner, I noticed that he was favoring his leg slightly. But now he had his game face on and it looked like he'd been nursing the same beer all night.

The evening's atmosphere settled into a nice mellow groove. Some people were playing guitars and singing while others were half-watching surf flicks and chatting. A small group was keeping the video game tournament going. Even the Aussies seemed under control, surely out of respect for Sid, who had to "work" tomorrow. But it was growing late and I was relieved when Josh and his teammates decided to leave. I walked them to their bungalows and on the way Josh confided to me that his leg was a little stiff. However, he said he was more worried about not having any of his favorite boards for the semi-finals.

I wasn't tired so I went back to the pavilion and ended up at a table with some of the older people, which in the surfing community means anybody over the age of 25. Among the group was Brazilian CEO Pedro Valiz who was getting drunker and louder by the minute. I could tell that Valiz was naturally gregarious but I'd also seen him be abusive towards Ellie and I assumed that kind of behavior wasn't a rarity for him. Valiz had procured a bottle of Arak and was drinking shots of it along with his beer. The booze had set him on the road to righteous indignation.

"The Brazilian team has done nothing wrong!" he practically yelled. "We're just surfing hard to show the world how good we really are. What went down with Rizo in the water today was an unfortunate accident. Could have happened to anyone."

Most of the crowd had cleared out and there was little danger of Valiz's remarks sparking a confrontation so I listened to what the man had to say, which was quite a lot. He knew I was somehow affiliated with White Sand and started talking in my direction.

"Whoever worked Bobby over should be drawn and quartered and then roasted over a spit."

Naturally, I agreed with him.

The two journalists who always seemed to be lurking in the background quietly pulled up chairs and sat down.

Pedro spread his arms out wide. "Sure, I admit I ask my team riders to surf hard. Maybe our ways aren't always entirely correct but we never do anything illegal and we would never intentionally hurt another surfer."

His speech was slurred. "Sam Woods is who you should worry about. We should all worry about that snake. He's responsible for all the problems we've had on tour this season. Woods is such a nice, easy going, mellow guy ... No! It's an act."

He paused to take another shot. He held the bottle out to me but I shook my head.

"The Hawaiians are always bad-mouthing the Brazilians to the Americans. But then they turn right around and denounce the Americans to the Brazilians. They're always trying to cause friction and fights to help themselves win the title."

With that, Valiz was done. "Think about it my friend," he said to me as he pushed back from the table. "Just think about it." Valiz was wasted but I had to admit I almost believed the guy. His remarks sounded sincere and people with things to hide don't usually sit down with the other side and spill their guts.

Back at my bungalow, I found Ellie sitting on the deck waiting for me. Lucky me.

She listened carefully as I replayed my conversation with Valiz. "There have been a lot of problems on tour this year," she said, "But if anybody's responsible it's Valiz, not Woods."

She got up. "Are you going to invite me inside or what?"

* * * * *

I was determined to be the first one in the water so the sun wasn't yet up when I left Ellie sleeping comfortably in my bed. I felt pretty good as I groped my way towards the coffee area. There's a lot to be said for only drinking beer. One big plus is that you hardly ever have a hangover to deal with the next morning — you really have to go big to work up a "beerover."

The morning session was a bit on the tricky side. The tide was so low I could clearly see the bottom on every takeoff so picking the right wave was critical to avoid hitting the reef. Eventually, a few other idiots joined me in the lineup. It was like playing Russian roulette out there — stroking into the wrong wave meant the very real possibility of serious bodily injury. I was relieved when the tide started to fill in but that's when I made the mistake of getting cocky. I kept paddling for a wave that I should have just let go. I got into it late and then had to wait for a stupid "sponge boarder" to punch through before I could make my bottom turn. I was blasted off my board and deposited tailbone-first onto the reef. I knew the impact was coming but there was nothing I could do about it. The wave had me in its grip and it was not letting go.

Fortunately, I landed on a flat spot so the impact wasn't so bad but then I was dragged against the reef and I could feel the skin being scraped off my back. My leash had held so my board was close at hand when I surfaced but I'd been pushed way inside and a long set of waves was now pounding across the reef. I kept trying to feel my back to determine the amount of damage; there was some blood but not a lot. There was no way I was going to let a little reef rash drive me from the water so I sat patiently and waited out the set and then stroked back out.

I'd been washed so far down the reef that it took me about 15 minutes to get back to the take off area where I found a horde of caffeinated surfers had arrived, jockeying for position and throwing each other the stink-eye stare.

I felt like someone had beaten me with a board but my back had stopped bleeding (a shark attack would have made the morning complete) so I tried to be positive and shortly thereafter I managed to pick off a couple of waves right out from under the nose of one of the Aussies who loved to call me "Rocky." He looked more than a little shaky and severely hung over so perhaps I had an unfair advantage. So what?

The lineup was getting more crowded by the minute, mostly with pros. It felt like time to begin my "G-Land drift" down the reef. The surf was still sizable, in the six-to-eight-foot range, but the waves were not all "makeable" by any means so wave selection was important. The power of the waves at G-Land is awesome, the good ones coming through resembled freight trains.

Here and there along the reef, pockets of surfers were trying for some of the less-crowded waves. As I drifted toward one such group, I recognized Sam Woods and two of his team members paddling and waiting for the next set. My first thought was to continue right past them but Sam had always been pleasant enough to me so I gave him the traditional Indonesian greeting, which he immediately returned. I could see Sam had also been bounced off the

153

reef this morning; there were several bright red scratches across his back.

"Looks like I'm not the only one who has a case of reef rash," I called to him.

Sam smiled. "My first wave of the day."

He had scars on his back as well. "Looks like you've had a lot of reef experience."

He laughed. "Oh, yeah, I've bounced off a few."

I thought his friends looked relieved when they realized I wasn't going to try and join them. After I passed them, I looked back and saw that they had all started paddling up the reef.

I refocused on my surf session and saw that there was a good section working a little farther down the reef so I picked out a landmark on the beach to stay located in the right area and surfed one stand-up barrel after another for the next three hours. Good times.

* * * * *

The first semi-final heat was underway when I got to the viewing stand. It was the Hawaiian, Chu, against the Brazilian, Pradratz. The surf was still off the charts for both size and quality. But the forecast was saying this would be the last day the organizers could count on consistently good surf so they scheduled the semis and the finals back-to-back.

Pradratz got out of the gate quickly with multiple rides on average-sized waves but Chu's tactic of waiting for the bigger, more impressive outside waves paid off and by the end of the half-hour heat he was clearly the winner.

The next match-up began immediately — Josh against Sid Barrow. At first, the waves were few and far between but soon waves began to show up with regularity and each surfer was able to pick and choose his wave. The heat was very close with each surfer matching the other wave for wave but in the end, Sid pulled out a victory. I couldn't help thinking that Josh's leg injury, coupled with not having his favorite boards, was the difference between winning and losing such a very close heat.

I hurried to get out to watch the final heat from the water. On the paddle out, I could feel the stiffness in my lower back. My back was sore from my collision with the reef but it was just a reminder that I was actually surfing a break that most people only dream about. The area adjacent to the lineup was packed with spectators in boats and every type of flotation device — from rubber rafts to canoes. The starter horn sounded and the final got underway.

Each final contestant was allowed a 30-minute waiting period from the end of the previous heat so Chu was more rested. But Sid was warmed up so it was hard to tell who had an advantage. The heat was a very close call; there were great waves and some outstanding surfing. Both surfers clocked substantial time in the green room. At the heat's conclusion, the spectators seemed evenly split as to the winner. The judges were totaling up the scorecards and the announcement would be made in the pavilion, amid much fanfare, as soon as everybody was in place.

Being a devious wave-crazed surfer, I took the opportunity to try for a few more rides. Things were going pretty good for the first hour or so; there were lots of waves and not many surfers. Occasionally, garbled loudspeaker noises followed by applause filtered out to the surf zone so I knew the awards ceremony was happening but I was more interested in catching my next wave than who was on top in the ratings. When the ceremony was over surfers started paddling out again. Chu won the contest, Barrow finished second, Pradratz third with Josh in fourth place.

When the sun set, I was still in the water surfing golden waves. No matter where else I traveled, I knew there would always only be one G-Land.

Chapter 12

HAWAII BECKONS

The next morning camp was chaos incarnate. The pros were eager to reach Hawaii's North Shore so they could prepare for the final contest of the year, the Pipeline Pro. Everyone seemed to be departing camp at the same time; thankfully, the staff ordered additional boats to accommodate all the surfboard bags, luggage, and bodies.

The Pipe Pro operates around a 10-day waiting period, which allows organizers to begin the contest when the swell and weather conditions are at their optimum. The White Sand team was booked on a 7:00 p.m. flight out of Bali. After a layover in Sydney, they'd arrive in Honolulu, Hawaii at 7:00 a.m. on Tuesday. There was no good reason that I could think of, or make up for that matter, for me to stay in Bali so I decided to leave with the team.

Ellie and I sat together for much of the flight so we had plenty of time to discuss the events of the past week. The fact that the Brazilian surfer had placed ahead of Josh was no surprise to her. She was convinced Pedro Valiz was the devil himself who had undoubtedly stolen Josh's boards and then had his surfer run Josh over.

"There have been 11 contests so far this season and that loud Brazilian has been involved in multiple incidents. The emotions in the water are crazy tense. It's so bad now that the Hawaiians won't stay at the same hotels as the Brazilians."

I floated the idea that the Hawaiians are also troublemakers but Ellie shook her head; her opinion of the Brazilians was set.

Going into Pipeline, the number-one slot in professional surfing was still up for grabs. Ellie had to resort to pen and paper to explain the point-rating system to me, but the results showed that Josh still had a slim chance. However, he would have to win the final contest outright so he was a long shot. We agreed that in this kind of competitive situation, Bobby would have had a much better chance.

The point spread between Chu, Barrow and Pradratz was so close that any of them could win it if he managed a top-three finish. It truly was all coming down to the final contest of the year.

Ellie took a long nap during the flight. The stress of constantly wrangling people and equipment, arranging accommodations and transportation and attending to the personal needs of the group had taken their toll and she used the transit time to recuperate.

For a surfer, the view during the descent into Honolulu Airport is inspirational — you can see Waikiki, Diamond Head and all the reefs. The surfers scattered about the white water, searching and waiting for the next wave, look tiny in the sea of crystal blue water.

Over the years, I've been to Oahu many times. Honolulu has always been the fast-paced big city where you hear the ever-present thump, thump, thump of the pile drivers working on another high-rise building foundation. But now the freeways are more crowded. The housing tracts have pushed out into previously undeveloped areas and the once raw and bawdy sections of town have become more "civilized."

It seems that the only thing that hasn't changed are the waves along the Kam Highway on Oahu's fabled North Shore. Known as "the seven-mile miracle," this stretch of coastline from Haleiwa to Velzyland offers some of the best surf in the world and attracts surfers from all over the globe. At this time each year, surfers want to prove to themselves, and others, that they are among the elite of surfing.

Hawaiian surf is not for everyone. The waves can be unbelievably powerful. The currents rage and so does the competition. The crowd factor alone is enough to discourage many surfers as it can sometimes take years just to gain enough respect to earn a spot in the lineup. A newcomer should never paddle out at any crowded Hawaiian break expecting to get good waves; it's a matter of respect for the locals. If a newcomer doesn't show respect, he can expect problems.

Traveling with the White Sand team certainly has its advantages. A three-van caravan was awaiting our arrival, but even so, getting all the people and equipment loaded was the usual hassle. We headed to Dolphin Bay Resort, where most everyone involved with the contest would surely be staying as it's the only sizeable hotel on the north end of the North Shore. Driving through Wahiawa, there were new buildings here and there and more people and traffic than I remembered but as the van began to head downhill and I could see the famous old arched Haleiwa Bridge, I started to feel right at home.

We drove on the coast road, which the locals call Kam highway. When we reached Laniakea, I was relieved to see there wasn't a swell — no surf meant I didn't have to hurry checking into the hotel. Our caravan passed by the legendary surf spots that are the stuff of dreams for surfers around the world: Chun's Reef, Waimea Bay, Backdoor, Off-The-Wall, Pipeline, Pupukea, Rocky Point, Kammie-land, Sunset and Velzyland.

Dolphin Bay Resort is a seven-story luxury hotel that rises from a point of land that fronts a beautiful blue lagoon. Development of this magnitude is out of place with the relatively quiet and rural atmosphere of the surrounding area but that doesn't stop the hotel from being popular with visiting surfers. Sure enough, when we arrived I heard staff tell Ellie that the hotel was sold out.

Ellie handed out the room keys, then got all the luggage and surfboards sorted out. Josh and I accompanied her to her room, where the first order of business was to check the weather, which looked promising. There was a low-pressure system building that looked like it might throw some swell in our direction, but nothing immediate.

Ellie checked her messages. Paul had called with the details on the Pipe beachfront house he had rented; it was near the house Koala Clothing Company had rented for the contest. Bobby's doctors gave him the okay to travel so he'd be arriving with Paul and would stay at the house. Wayne was set to arrive with Josh's new quiver of seven boards tomorrow at 2:00 p.m.

"Paul asked us all to be careful," Ellie said, looking at Josh.

Josh sighed, obviously tired of the concern for his safety. Before he could tell Ellie for the millionth time that he could take care of himself, I diffused the situation by inviting him to go with me for a surf check, just to unwind, since we knew there was no surf anyway.

Ellie gave me a key to one of the vans. We loaded our boards, just in case, and were soon cruising back towards Haleiwa. I stopped several times to show Josh some of the lesser-known spots that only break on the right swell. We also hit Kammie's Market and picked up a case of Primo, the local brew.

"We're going to make a quick visit to an old friend of mine," I told Josh. "I don't want to show up empty-handed."

Stan Kwyjec has lived in and around Haleiwa for at least 30 years. He moved to Hawaii as a young man and never left. From one rental house to another, he's always managed to remain near the surf along the seven-mile stretch. Stan is a small guy, dark-complexioned with black hair and brown eyes. He's told me he's Polish but the Hawaiians treat him as one of their own. When he stands next to a group of big locals, it's almost comical. He looks like a little kid, but he speaks their language. Whatever he has, which usually isn't much, he shares. He gets by making and selling craft items and performing odd jobs and he usually has roommates to help cover the rent. Stan knows everyone on the North Shore, which even today is a tightly knit community where everyone knows everyone else's business.

Josh and I found Stan sitting on his veranda with three local Hawaiians. They were drinking beers and telling stories.

"Holy shit!" Josh said as I was parking the van. "Do you know who those guys are?"

"Yep. Tiger Esperanza, Junior Kalimaki and Titus Jones."

"Wow."

All three are North Shore surfing legends and they've done just about everything there is to do from 25-foot Waimea to third reef Pipe. Stan walked down to greet us.

Josh looked like he wasn't going to be able to talk for awhile so after I introduced him to everyone, I cracked a beer, gave it to him and pointed toward a chair.

Everybody agreed that the next big swell would arrive soon. "It's been a good winter so far," Tiger said. "Consistent and not too many flat spells."

There are certain times when I feel it's appropriate to break my drinking rule and have a beer on a weekday and this was one of those times. I hadn't seen these guys in awhile and it was important to get off on the right foot.

"How's Bobby?" Junior asked.

The question threw me but then Junior explained he and Bobby are in-laws. Junior's sister is married to Bobby's uncle. This was news to me.

All three Hawaiians pumped me for information but I had to tell them that no arrests had been made. "Bobby's doing better. He'll be here for the contest, staying at the White Sand house."

The guys were riled up about the attack. Apparently, Bobby has quite the North Shore fan club. I make it a rule not to tell people my business so I didn't explain that I was working for Paul Maguire on the "case" and I changed the subject.

"Hey, Stan, do you still go to the airport offering free rides to tourist girls just off the plane?"

That got everybody laughing because it was true, Stan had been a real dog in his younger days. Even now, two rooms in his place were rented out to "haole" girls. We drank some more beers and I tried to get the guys to open up a little for Josh's benefit.

They have countless stories of near-death experiences over 20-plus years of surfing the North Shore. I did manage to get a few stories out of them because I know the right questions to ask but to them it's no big deal; the danger just goes with the territory.

Junior brought out his ukulele for a couple of tunes and insisted that we sing along. He knew we didn't know the words but nobody cared. Josh and I did the best we could and it reminded me of many years ago, during my first trips to Oahu, when I stumbled along to the same songs around a beach campfire. Ah, the Aloha spirit.

It was close to dinner time and since Tiger, Junior and Titus are all family guys, they needed to get home so we said our goodbyes. Josh walked with them to the gate. He had overcome his shyness and was trying to get tips on the best way to surf Pipeline. I don't think he realized he was wasting his time — these Hawaiians would be rooting for Butch Chu.

Once we were alone, I told Stan as much background as I thought necessary to give him a full understanding of what I was trying to accomplish, namely figuring out who was responsible for the attacks on the elite surfers of the Pro Tour. I explained about Dede Betet, Harvey Patel and the Brotherhood connection and mentioned our theory about the clothing companies as well.

"Those PAB guys are getting to be a real pain in the ass," Stan said. "They come by once a week. They won't take no for an answer, probably because they've made so many converts on the North Shore. Somebody told me Chu is PAB now."

Stan made the statement very causally but for me this was huge news.

"You know Stan, if Chu is a member of the Brotherhood it could throw a whole new light on what's been happening lately. Are you sure?"

"I heard it from someone at the beach. Give me some time and I'll check it out and let you know one way or the other."

"Thanks. But please remember, Stan, keep everything low key. We don't want to let people know that we're interested in the PAB or Chu."

On the way back to the hotel, it looked like there might be the beginnings of a swell starting to fill in, a good sign for a morning surf session. Josh told me about the Pipe lineup "tips" he got from the guys. He'd only surfed Pipe at average size so I had to tell him that if he followed their advice, he'd be annihilated in the shore break and would never even make it outside.

"When the wave size and swell direction change, everything about the break is affected. Don't worry, though, because all the competitors will be in the same boat. Pipe doesn't discriminate." I laughed and so did Josh.

The odds were definitely against Josh coming back to win the title — any of the other three surfers had a better chance — but we still had to be careful. I asked him to stay close to other surfers and his teammates until we could get a handle on exactly where the threat was coming from.

Back at the hotel, with Josh was out of harm's way, at least for the rest of the day, I "relaxed" in my room. Staring out at the blue Pacific, I went over the situation in my mind and considered the options. We know the Brotherhood is involved to some degree, but just who or how much is still unknown. Now, if I look at the clothing companies, my primary suspect has to be Pedro Valiz. But Sam Woods and Steve Reynolds also deserve consideration.

"So they're all suspects," I said aloud.

But on second thought, Reynolds doesn't seem like a viable suspect since he and his team came to our rescue during the attack in Kuta Beach.

The company owners are the people with the most to gain and greed is always a good motive. Whoever is responsible has a far reach — Bobby was attacked in Baja; Arrington died in northern California; and Josh was jumped in Indonesia — and they're neat and tidy; not a lot of loose ends for me to pick up on, that's for sure.

When Stan mentioned Chu as a possible Brotherhood member it was like a finger pointing accusingly at the apparently easygoing Woods. I called Ellie and asked her to select some team members to find out on the sly whether Valiz, Woods or Reynolds or anyone associated with them has PAB connections. This whole thing started with the PAB and if I can tie anybody in with the religious group, at least I'll have a direction to follow.

I went down to the lobby and arranged for a minivan rental and then wandered around a bit. I've been to

Dolphin Bay before, but not as a guest. I usually stay either with friends or at one of the smaller places along the North Shore. Dolphin Bay is massive — hundreds of rooms, several bars and restaurants, two pools lined with cabanas, a golf course and miles of beachfront. Nice digs for sure but I still feel more at home sitting on Stan's front porch drinking a Primo than I ever would sitting poolside at Dolphin Bay with a Mai-Tai in hand.

Surfers were checking into the hotel in a steady stream and the lobby was full of surfboard travel bags. The new arrivals were the total opposite of many of the guests — Iowa farmers on vacation to escape the blizzards of the Great Plains.

I went up to Ellie's room. She'd been following the weather reports; a definite swell on the way and the word was out that the contest start was looking more and more likely. She invited me to a dinner hosted by the local White Sand big wigs but that was the last thing I felt like doing, so I begged off.

I had a restless night's sleep. I couldn't turn off my thoughts that ran — like the flickering frames of one of those old-time silent movies — in a loop through my mind. Finally, I got up and started roaming around the room. I took out my Magic Frye and rubbed on a little more wax. I admired its shape, outline, and rocker and wondered if this board would launch me into some epic surf over the next few days. I went out on to the deck and closed my eyes against the trade winds blowing in my face, the same dependable winds that for centuries have filled the sails of seafaring men of every nation. The breeze smelled of sea, salt, sun and moist earth.

I try not to worry about things beyond my control but this whole situation felt like a painful long-forgotten memory that's trying to claw its way to the surface of my mind.

165

Yet just when the answer to the riddle is almost within my grasp, it flits away.

At the first hint of dawn, I cruised down the Kam Highway to a spot that was like an old friend, a place where I've spent many enjoyable days. At one time, in my younger years, it was almost a secret spot but nowadays nowhere is safe from the wave-hungry crowds. West of Haleiwa is an easily accessible stretch of beach with a wide variety of breaks to choose from. As the early morning dimness gradually gave way, I could see small, well-shaped peaks breaking in several locations on the offshore reef. For my first Hawaiian surf this trip, and because the swell was small, it seemed appropriate that I ride my fun-shaped Pineapple model. Soon, I was paddling out into the amazingly clear blue waters of Oahu.

* * * * *

The waves were small, fun, consistent, and still uncrowded, which suited me just fine. I needed to clear my head and surfing can almost always make me forget my problems. A rhythmic pattern developed governed by the consistent pulse of waves, tide and the slight wind blowing into the wave faces. It wasn't long before I was doing my word repetition routine. I never try to analyze these random words or numbers but as soon as I started on today's word, "lelipi," I realized that repeating my newly acquired Indonesian word for snake didn't feel random. I spelled "lelipi" again and again and then said the word to myself syllable-by-syllable: le-li-pi, le-li-pi, le-li-pi, doing a mental chant of sorts and trying to analyze how the word reflects its definition.

Wait a second.

During Pedro Valiz's drunken ramblings in the dining area at G-Land, he called Sam Woods a snake. "Sam

Woods is who you should worry about," he had said. "We should all worry about that snake."

When I was in Medewi, the village elders described a peculiar scar on little Sammy Patel's back as the reason for his nickname of "little snake" and said that nobody knew his true last name.

When I paddled by Woods in the G-Land lineup and saw his badly scarred back, one of those scars had an "S" shape.

When I was walking to the dining area at the surf camp, I passed by Woods and heard him speaking fluent Indonesian. Woods had indicated to me he didn't understand Indonesian. Another lie.

This whole thing started, when a one-time employee of one of Woods subsidiary wetsuit companies, Brother Elias, had under orders from an Indonesian, Dede Betet, caused the kidnapping of Bobby Contraras.

The pieces fit into the puzzle. It was very likely that Sam Woods is Harvey Patel's half brother Sammy and lifelong friend to Dede Betet. Finally, If my hunch was right, I'd found the living breathing missing link between the PAB and a clothing company. Together, the PAB and Third Reef were responsible for the conspiracy that resulted in murder and vicious attacks. Now, the snake had to be drawn out into the open and stopped.

Surfing was no longer an option so I rode a wave in, toweled off, and jumped in the van. As I drove, I went over it all again to make sure I hadn't missed something. The more I thought about it the more my early morning surf ephphany seemed right on. But I needed to make sure I couldn't poke any holes in my own theory before I started spreading the news.

* * * * *

I stopped by Stan's on the way back to the hotel. He was sitting on the porch working on some bamboo pipes for the tourist trade. He greeted me with, "I've got good news and bad news. What do you want to hear first?"

"I'm off to a good start this morning so let's go with the good."

"Third Reef's number one rider Butch Chu is born again PAB. And if that's not enough for you, Sam Woods has been quietly financing the Brotherhood here in the Islands for many, many years."

"Well, Stanley me boy, your good news has just made my morning complete. I'll get into the reasons in a minute but first let me have the bad news — I don't want to get too cocky."

"The word is out all over the North Shore that if your boy Josh or Barrow or Pradratz show up at any of the local breaks they are to be taken out."

"Taken out? What does that mean?"

"Run over, beaten up — use your imagination, you know what can happen. Someone, nobody knows who, started a rumor that those three contest surfers are saying that they're the only ones who can really handle Hawaiian power. You know the locals aren't going to stand for that kind of disrespect at their home breaks. It's a matter of pride."

Surfing can be a very competitive sport; there are too many people and too few waves. People who consistently surf a particular break feel entitled to some degree of "ownership" of that break. This phenomenon is called "localism" and it's present to some degree at most surf spots. Hawaii's localism can be off the charts and for a proud Hawaiian surfer there's no greater insult than being "called out" by a bunch of traveling pros.

I held my finger up to Stan for a timeout while I got Ellie on the phone. "Ellie I've got quite a bit to tell you but, first, have you heard a rumor going around the beach that Josh and some other pros are talking trash about the locals?"

"No, I've been cooped-up in my room all morning. What's going on?"

"I'm over at Stan's and he's telling me if Josh, Barrow or Pradratz paddle out at the local breaks there will be trouble. You'd better sit on Josh and start making phone calls. I'll be back at the hotel in half an hour."

This could get ugly real quick.

"Well, Stanley, this is a fine mess you've got me into," I said jokingly. "Seriously, though, Josh was so impressed with meeting Tiger and the guys the other night — you saw him, he couldn't talk for 20 minutes. I know Barrow is equally respectful and even Pradratz, who can be a real ass in the water, isn't dumb enough to bad-mouth the locals. This rumor is a pack of lies."

"You don't have to convince me, Mike, but I'm not the problem. The only way to diffuse this situation is to get everybody together and talk it out. If the Hawaiians aren't convinced that those three aren't talking trash, there is going to be trouble. I'll start talking to people about a sit down, but it's up to you and the contest organizers to make this meeting happen. Everyone needs this biggest contest of the year to go off without a bunch of fighting and hassling."

"All right, as soon as I get back to the hotel I'm going to dump this whole thing in Ellie's lap. She's the one with the contest connections."

Before leaving, I gave Stan a quick rundown of my theory that Sam Woods is Harvey Patel's half brother. As my man on the ground, embedded in the community, keeping Stan informed just makes sense.

"If Woods and Patel are related then it would sure explain a lot, but how can you know for sure?"

I could tell by the look on Stan's face that he was just getting started discussing this new information, but I had to move. "Don't worry, I'm all over it. I've got to get back to the hotel and get things in motion but I'll call as soon as I know more."

By the time I got back to Dolphin Bay, and knocked on Ellie's door, the worst had already happened.

"Pradratz was out surfing Velzyland, doing his usual slash and burn and cutting out the other surfers when one of the locals decided he'd had enough. The guy beat the daylights out of Pradratz on the beach. Then he broke his board in half, and just for good measure wrapped his surf leash around his neck. Luckily, a lifeguard came by and cooled everything out and took Pradratz for medical attention."

"No doubt Pradratz can be really obnoxious in the water but it sounds like overkill to me. Stan thinks he can get the locals to come in for a meeting to try to straighten things out before anyone else gets hurt. Can you talk to the contest organizers about holding a meeting where everyone can have their say and hopefully clear the air?"

"I swear if it's not one thing, it's another. I don't even have time to take care of team business anymore. I thought all I was going to have to do was keep Josh in one piece until the contest started and now we have a whole new situation to deal with. But in answer to your question, yes, I'll talk to organizers right away. The professional tour cannot afford to have the biggest contest of the year sabotaged by a bunch of false rumors."

"Before you get started on that, Ellie, I've got something else to tell you. I was out in the water this morning, just letting all this stuff run through my head, when everything just fell into place. Remember when I told you that Patel's half brother Sammy, the one he grew up with, had the nickname of little snake because of an "S" shaped scar on his back? Well, Sam Woods has that scar. I saw it when we were surfing G-Land. I also just found out from Stan that Sam Woods has been quietly connected to the PAB for years and that Chu is a recently converted member."

As I talked, it became very important to me to convince Ellie that my theory was correct so I just kept laying it on.

She finally cut me off. "All right already, I get the picture and I have to admit that what you're saying makes a lot of sense. One thing I have to say about you, you're never dull."

"We now know both those guys are PAB and with Chu as the world's number-one surfer, Sam's clothing sales will go through the roof and the Brotherhood will pick up new members by the truckload. We have to find out if I'm right about Sam's true identity. The only way I see to confirm it is to talk with the people in the village of Medewi. I'm going to e-mail Steve Roper on Bali and have him send Rizal back to the village with a picture of Woods."

While I worked on my e-mail to Roper, I asked Ellie if she wanted to update Paul. She was talking on the phone so she mouthed the words "You do it" while pointing at me at the same time. I was due at the airport to pick up Wayne very soon so I wrote Paul a short and sweet e-mail:

"Paul, something big is breaking here. We think Sam Woods is Harvey Patel's half brother from Indo. We are trying to confirm his identity. PLEASE TAKE NO ACTION ON YOUR END UNTIL WE ARE CERTAIN. I THINK I HAVE A PLAN. Meanwhile, there's a lot of friction right now on the North Shore between the contest and locals. Ellie is trying to organize a meeting to diffuse the situation. We will advise when we know more."

Ellie ended her call and threw the phone on the bed. "Don't worry too much about keeping Paul in the loop, Mike. He calls me about every 20 minutes."

"Good. Make sure he doesn't do anything about this new information until it's confirmed. I think I have a plan."

She looked at me with a "What now?" expression but I was done talking. If I didn't break too many speed limits, I could still be on time to pick up Wayne from the airport.

Chapter 13

THE SEVEN-PART PLAN

I was really glad to see Wayne. The guy is a rock; nothing fazes him and that's exactly the kind of person I needed to help me bring this case to a close.

While we waited by the luggage carousel, I started updating him on the entire story, including the current powder keg situation on the North Shore. Wayne was particularly interested in the nighttime Kuta beach melee but he was disappointed that I hadn't used any of the defensive techniques he taught me. "If you'd been training correctly, your reactions would have been instinctive. You're definitely going to have to spend more time in the gym."

By the time we lugged all seven surfboards to the minivan, Wayne was pretty much up to speed on things so I launched into the pitch for my plan. "I've got an idea on how to expose Sam Woods and I need your help. How would you like to play the part of a hit man for hire?"

"Huh?"

"We need someone to approach Woods and offer to take out one of the top contest surfers so his guy, Butch Chu, can win the contest."

"So, what, I'm just supposed to walk up to him and ask him if he wants me to kill Sid Barrow?"

Wayne has a way of getting right to the heart of the matter. "No. First of all, we're talking hurting or disabling, not killing, so get that thought out of your mind. We'll do a lot of careful preparation so that when you finally meet Sam Woods in person it'll already be a done deal."

"You make it sound simple. But what if I say the wrong thing?"

Well, how about that? I found a crack in the rock. I'd never heard Wayne sound nervous before. "Trust me Wayne, you're perfect for this job. All you have to do is act natural. If I'm right about Woods, he wants this so bad that he won't suspect a thing."

I felt a little guilty about doing such a hard sell on Wayne, but while anyone would agree that he would make a perfect hit man, it was crucial that Wayne believed he could pull it off because if Woods sensed something was wrong, he'd walk away from the offer, and our trap.

"Okay, I'm in. Who knows? Maybe this role will launch my new career."

I started up the van. "As a hit man?"

Wayne raised his fist and I cowered over the steering wheel, laughing. "No, as an actor. So what's next, boss?"

"Well, we can't have you seen around the North Shore so we're going to check you into a hotel in town until we get everything organized."

After I reassured Wayne that his stay in town would only be for a few days, he agreed. I used one of Paul's lines on him. "Hey, maybe you'll get some surf."

We found a room at a nice beachfront hotel in the Waikiki area. I gave Wayne my credit card and some cash and then headed back to Dolphin Bay. The 45-minute drive gave me time to go over everything again; the plan was looking pretty good.

As I drove past the various breaks on the Kam Highway, I saw signs of some "swellular" activity beginning to kick in. There would be surf soon, maybe even enough for the Pipe Pro to be held.

As soon as I got back to my hotel room, I called Steve Roper in Uluwatu, Bali.

Steve picked up on the third ring. "Who's calling?"

Before I could answer, he followed with, "Do you have any idea how early it is?"

I had completely forgotten about the time difference. While he chewed me out, I apologized a few times. Finally, I got a chance to ask my questions.

"Have you had a chance to read my e-mail yet?"

"Mike, you just woke me up out of a sound sleep. What do you think? So, you want to tell me? Or you want me to read the email and call you back?"

"Sorry, man. It's real straightforward. If you can do it, no need to call me back until you have something. I wouldn't be asking if it wasn't important so please give it your best shot."

"You're starting to freak me out. Did somebody die or something?"

"No, no, but we're trying to make sure it doesn't come to that."

"Okay, okay. I'm on it. Bye."

I do have a tendency to micro-manage. But in construction, you can always count on half your sub-contractors to not do what they say they will, so confirming phone calls go with the territory.

Ellie answered her cell phone on the first ring. I told her Josh's boards had arrived safe and sound and could be picked up anytime from the minivan in the parking garage. Then, I asked her to meet me by the pool for a plan meeting.

"Yep. I'll see you in 10."

It was time to reveal part three of my seven-part plan. Part one was Steve Roper working to confirm Sam Woods's identity. Part two had been securing Wayne's role as the hit man for hire. I had no clue how to accomplish part three but I was betting Ellie could guide me.

"We need someone who can set up audio video surveillance for our sting operation. Someone we can rely on to keep the plan quiet and monitor the sting — details of time and place to be determined."

"The only guy who comes to mind is James Blakely. He does all the contest web casts so this is right up his alley. How much can I tell him?"

"There's no use holding anything back. We can't expect the guy to operate in the dark. But make sure he understands he can't talk to anybody about this."

"Okay, I'll give him a try."

I went over my entire hair-brained scheme with her and she liked it. "In fact, I love the plan, Mike. But there's no way it's going to work."

At this point, I could only share her pessimism. The key component of the plan was still missing — the right person to draw the snake out from under his rock and into the open. "I'm working on finding the right guy to approach Woods."

As for the business about the ridiculous rumor floating around, Ellie had pulled together all the players needed to put an end to it. Everyone agreed that a face-to-face meeting was the only way to clear the air and diffuse the tension between the visiting pros and the local Hawaiians. A conference room at the hotel was reserved for tomorrow at 1:00 p.m. — low tide, of course, since attendees couldn't be expected to miss any surf.

I called Stan, who for the first time actually answered his phone, and gave him the meeting time and place. I agreed to pick him up at his house and chauffeur him around to help spread the word about the meeting.

While I was on the phone, Ellie stood up and stretched and then walked toward the many vacationers lounging by the pool. I'm sure she was wishing she could trade places with any of them.

When I got off the phone, she came back to the table. "Paul and Bobby are flying in day after tomorrow. Paul promised not do anything to jeopardize the plans we're working on. He also said he wants Sam Woods and Harvey Patel to go down in flames. Okay, I'm off to get in touch with Blakely."

I knew I was getting ahead of myself by putting part three of my plan into action. The safe bet was to wait and get confirmation from Bali confirming Sam Woods's identity but I didn't want to waste any time. Plus, I really felt that I was right about Woods. So, I decided to proceed to part four of the plan.

I was relying on Stan for help in finding somebody to approach Woods. I needed someone whom Woods could trust completely. That someone was going to tell Woods about a hit man who would, for a comparatively small fee, rough up Barrow, Pradratz or Josh so that they'd have to drop out of the contest.

As Stan and I drove around beach parking lots and then stopped in at local markets and ramshackle houses to spread the word about the meeting, we brainstormed about the right person to use to contact Woods. At first, Stan suggested Junior Kalimaki but then relented because too many people know he's related to Bobby Contraras.

"Who else, Stan? Who would be willing to work with us to expose Sam Woods?"

"I have somebody in mind, but let me think on it for awhile." All the balls were now in the air; all I had to do now was make sure I was there to catch them when they came down.

* * * * *

The situation with the Hawaiians was more complicated than it appeared. Of course, the Hawaiians are loyal to their "brahs" first and foremost against all comers but there's also an old rift that continues to split the

Hawaiians into different factions: the locals who surf the pro circuit, traveling up to 40,000 miles annually to contest venues all over the world, and their supporters on one side and on the other, the locals who specialize in surfing the famous North Shore spots but can't compete in contests because they're not on the circuit. In years past, "stay-at-home locals" resented not being allowed to surf in contests on the North Shore, spots that they considered to be theirs by right, while the traveling pros felt people should have to participate in the pro tour and earn their way into the local contests.

The Hawaiian contests are now open to deserving non-pro surfers who have proven their worth at places like Sunset and Pipeline. But resentment between the factions still exists and could possibly surface at the meeting, muddying the waters and potentially preventing a resolution to the current situation.

Stan suggested one last stop on the meeting notification route. "Actually, Mike, this guy could be your best bet to hook Woods."

I stayed in the car as Stan went to the front door of an older dilapidated house. When the door opened, I recognized Titus Jones. Stan went inside and I watched kids, dogs, and even a couple of chickens run around in the front yard. After several minutes, Stan stepped back outside and waved to me.

Titus and I have surfed together and hung out many times over the years. I consider him a friend but I realized this whole story was pretty weird so I was just hoping he would give me a fair hearing.

Inside, a young guy named Makua was sitting next to Titus at the kitchen table. I recognized him as an up and coming surfer. Titus introduced him as his wife's brother. Stan introduced him as a PAB initiate.

"Stan told us the whole deal and what you're trying to put together," said Titus. I took a seat at the table and retold the entire tale because everything depended on getting these guys on my side. I kept coming back to Bobby's crippling and Ramon's death.

"If Woods is responsible for what happened to those guys then he deserves anything he gets," said Titus. "Besides, all he has to do to prove he's innocent is say no to the hit man offer and walk away. No problem."

"Exactly."

Makua didn't look so sure. After all, he was being asked to betray a respected elder in his newly-adopted church. "Listen, Makua, we aren't going to do anything until we hear back from Bali. So just do me a favor and think about what I've said. If Woods is who we think he is then I hope you'll help us expose him. If it turns out he's innocent then I'll apologize for wasting everybody's time."

Stan and I got up to leave.

Titus already knew about the meeting. "I'll be there."

With that, we all shook hands and Stan and I headed out into the humid Hawaiian evening.

Back at the hotel, Ellie's room had turned into command central, complete with bulletin boards, computers, and the constant ringing of cell phones. Several team members and a couple of clothing reps were tracking a well-advertised storm developing offshore in the Pacific. The hope was that when the swell hit, the contest would be on.

Ellie and I went into the bedroom where she told me what she'd been able to gather from her team members and other sources. "Valiz is a Catholic. Nobody seems to know personal details on Reynolds but he does have a reputation as a partier so it doesn't make sense for him to be PAB since they believe in abstinence."

"Pretty much what I figured. So we're down to Sam Woods again. I think Stan and I found the right person to approach him, this kid Makua, but he won't commit until we know for sure about Woods. Damn, I wish Steve would call."

Ellie had news of her own. "I talked John Blakely into helping us with the surveillance, if and when it happens. I had to tell him everything and he was pretty blown away. I made him promise not to say anything but you know what they say, if more than one person knows, it's not a secret."

"Yeah, it's starting to bother me that so many people know what we're up to but that's beyond our control."

"Blakely's an electronics genius and he's used to working from a tent on the beach, so he's perfect for this gig. He says he needs at least two hours notice."

"Nice work, Ellie. Thanks."

Everybody seemed to gravitate towards Ellie's room that night with the usual drinking and carrying on. The meeting, which everyone was calling "the summit," was the big topic of conversation. Blakely dropped by and we stepped out on the balcony for a private conversation.

"Ellie says you're good people, Mike, and that you can be trusted. Otherwise, I wouldn't have anything to do with this kind of business. Woods is a big player on the pro tour. If something goes wrong, I could lose my job."

"Right now there are only a handful of people who have any idea about what's going on. Before we do anything we'll be 100-percent sure."

"Okay. Like I told Ellie, I can set up fast but I'm hoping for an inside location because outdoors presents far more problems. Man, I still can't believe this is really happening. If your plan works, it's going to turn the surfing world upside down."

That thought had already crossed my mind but hearing Blakely say it out loud made me nervous. I managed to push it out of my mind as we walked back inside the busy room.

*   *   *   *   *

The morning dawned grey and windy. The chances of surfing were just about zero so I killed time before "the summit" by undergoing a thorough workout in the gym followed by a run on the beach and a swim in the lagoon. Then I hit the sauna, took a shower and ate a healthy breakfast. For the entire morning and right up to the meeting time, I was going over "what if?" scenarios in my mind and working out alternatives for different situations should they occur. But I knew that ultimately everything depended on just how badly Woods wanted to be number one.

The meeting began as scheduled with the main contest organizer and many respected elder statesmen of surfing, both local and "hoale," sitting around a conference table. Stan's drinking buddies Junior and Tiger were among the group. There were many people in the crowded room who had something to say but the most important speakers were Josh and Sid Barrow. Both vehemently denied making any disparaging comments about local North Shore surfers. Pradratz was either too injured or too embarrassed to attend so, for once, Valiz stepped up and did the right thing.

"Nobody who has anything to do with my company or our surf team has said anything to run down Hawaiian surfing. We all know you guys are the best out here on the North Shore and we have nothing but respect for your surfing ability. I am just sorry that these false rumors led to Pietro being attacked."

The denials had the desired effect. Everyone who had something to say had a chance at the microphone and the

181

contest's head honcho stressed that 23 local surfers were entered into the contest, something the circuit only allows in Hawaii as a sign of respect for the level of surfing ability found in the Islands. The locals seemed appeased. Almost all the visiting pros were in attendance and quite an effort was made to have everybody in the room shake hands as the meeting came to a close. No one present could, or would, say anything definitive about where the rumors originated but everyone knew a bullet had been dodged. Now, the contest could proceed without the fear of contestants being attacked.

During the meeting, Stan and I stood against the rear wall. Neither of us had felt a need to make any comments. I also noticed Sam Woods and his guys said nothing but I was certain this whole confrontational mess was his plan. Just another attempt on his part to take out the opposition and clear the way for Butch Chu.

There was talk that Pradratz had sustained a serious injury and that he might even be scratched from the contest. Josh was a severe underdog in the contest so if any further attacks were planned, Sid Barrow was the logical target. I hoped the Aussies were taking precautions.

My cell phone rang as I was getting ready to drive Stan back to Haleiwa.

"Steve Roper here, calling from the Magic Island Kingdom of Bali. Your good buddy Rizal just got back from a very quick trip to a small village called Medewi. You want to talk to him or do you want me to give you the bad news?"

It felt like my stomach had just dropped down below my knees. "Just tell me, Steve. My blood pressure is about to enter the danger zone."

"Okay. The bad news is that this is going to cost you and Paul a brand new wardrobe for my man, Rizal. And I'll take one, too. The other news is that Sam Woods used to go by the nickname of 'Little Snake.'"

I laughed. "You dog! I was dying over here."

"Sorry, Mike, I couldn't resist. Rizal said he showed the picture to the same group of village elders whom you talked to and they all confirmed that Woods is Harvey Patel's older half-brother, Sammy."

"Steve, you and Rizal really pulled through for us. Thanks a million. The clothes will be in the mail and email me a bill for your time and trouble and I'll get you paid. We still need to keep this quiet for a few more days so not a word to anyone, okay?"

"You got it. My lips are sealed."

I breathed a sigh of relief. My gamble on the fact that I knew who Sam Woods really was had paid off. Finally, after I'd traveled halfway around the world, all the missing links were found and connected and all the main players officially identified. Now, it was time to make them pay.

Stan and I drove straight to Titus's house. When we pulled up, he was just getting out of his car. We told him that word from Bali positively identified Woods.

"Okay, I'll get Makua going as soon as I can."

"Do you want us to stick around until Makua gets home, to talk to him?" I asked.

"No, I'll do it. To be honest, you guys will probably just make him nervous. Give me a chance to talk him around. He'll be okay."

We briefly went over a few approaches that Makua could take with Woods. The main points were that the hit man for hire was a mainlander not known on the Island. Makua had met him at the gym. He would take out anybody for $10,000, and he was flying home very soon, so time was short. The meeting between the hit man and Woods should take place indoors, either at someone's house or a hotel. It would be up to Makua to use the best approach to entice Woods to take the bait and set the meeting. We all felt that offering up a mainlander, who was soon leaving town would appeal to Woods because there would appear to be less chance that the deed could be traced back to him. There was also another factor that might help things along: Since peace had been made at "the summit" Woods would be looking for another way to eliminate the competition.

The early morning storm had passed, leaving patchy white clouds with occasional bursts of sunshine in its wake. On the drive to Stan's house, we saw scattered surfers in the water. The first pulse of the eagerly-anticipated swell had arrived.

Stan invited me to relax a while on his porch. First, I had some calls to make to spread the news from Steve Roper. Ellie said she'd let Blakely know that all systems were go. Next, I called Wayne. He, of course, wanted to come out to the North Shore ASAP. I told him to continue enjoying his Waikiki vacation for a little while longer. I called Paul last because I knew he'd need a minute to vent.

"So this whole mess is thanks to the two things in the world that have caused probably more suffering than anything else: greed and religion. We got Woods cashing in big time in the clothing market while Patel gets worldwide recognition and converts to the PAB. What a pair. It's kind of hard to tell where one starts and the other leaves off. And they've been working together this whole time calling the shots while the rest of us have been playing catch-up. The scope of this thing is unbelievable. To think these two slimy worms planned all this and the worst part is that they came so close to getting away with it. Okay, now that I've got that out of my system tell me about this plan I've been hearing about. I hope it's a good one."

"The plan, in a nutshell, is for Woods to go on the worldwide web and confess to being a lowlife scum."

I went over the details.

"It could work. Let's give it a try. I want you to know that even if nothing else goes right from here on out, I'm really happy with the job you've done on this, Mike, and one way or another, we're going to make these guys pay."

"Thanks Paul, I appreciate the vote of confidence."

"You got it, buddy. Hey, I was talking with Bobby earlier and he called you "the surf detective." What do you think about that? Pretty good, right?

I laughed. "Surf detective, yeah, I like that. Maybe I'm the very first of its kind."

"Bobby and I are flying out in the morning. We'll see you at the Pipe house tomorrow night. Good luck. You're going to need it."

Stan and I kicked back on his porch and talked about old times and discussed the changes back on the mainland and here in Oahu. We laughed about how broke we were during our first trip to the Islands. Our version of going out to dinner was to cruise the area and pick papayas, mangos, and lychee nuts from the neighbor's trees. On special occasions we'd make a can of Campbell's Cream of Mushroom Soup and tuna fish over rice. While we talked, a few passersby on the quiet dirt road waved or called out a greeting. The laid-back country feeling still exists on the North Shore. You just have to know where to find it.

Before I left Stan's house, I told him I'd have my cell phone within reach 24/7. "Call me when you hear from Titus or Makua."

Back at the hotel, I checked in with Ellie who was, as usual, parked in front of her laptop. She immediately started in with the surf report, which was definitely indicating a building northwest swell. Everyone had been put on notice for a likely Saturday start for the contest. I tried to relax and hang around with Ellie, but my nerves were stretched tight while waiting to hear from Makua. Waiting is one of my least favorite things.

I spent a restless night but as it turned out, I did not have to wait for a phone call after all. I saw the entire conversation between Makua and Woods take place the following morning on the beach at Pipeline.

I was up at my usual early hour and had already done quite a bit of driving along the Kam Highway, looking for a good spot to paddle out. I ended up walking down the well-worn path to the beach at Pipeline. The famous peak was beginning to work with the normal pack of surfers all hoping for just one wave to themselves. The scaffolding for the judge's stand was being erected as well as some tent structures in preparation for the contest. As I continued to scan the activity on the beach, I saw a small group of surfers standing near the area where people usually start their paddle out. Upon closer inspection, it turned out to be Sam Woods and his Third Reef crew holding a team meeting before paddling out for a warm-up session. The waves were getting larger with each new set of waves generated by the far-off Pacific storm. I relocated to an area farther up the beach and backed up towards the palms and ferns that line the beach to give myself some cover. The beach meeting broke up a short time later and all the surfers headed into the water. As Woods stood watching, I saw Makua approach him. It was not a long conversation but they started to walk as they talked and they left the beach together.

By this time, the beach was a beehive of activity as more and more people began work on different projects. Blakely had arrived and was supervising the setup of his web cast tent. I stood mesmerized by the beautiful sight of Pipeline's inside-out tubes peeling down the reef. Even with the large crowd in the water, many waves went unridden — a testament to this break being considered one of the most difficult in the world to master. After a good half-hour had elapsed since Makua left the beach, I called him. When he answered, I could hear many voices in the background so I asked if it was okay to talk.

"No problem, I'm at Titus's house."

"I saw you talking to Woods on the beach at Pipe. Did you ask him?"

"Yeah, I finally did but it was real hard to figure out a way to bring up the subject. I started out by asking him if he thought I could make it onto the Third Reef surf team. We've talked about that before so it wasn't a weird question to ask. I told him how hard I'd been working out in the water and in the gym to get myself into top shape. Then he gave me the opening I needed. He said he didn't have time to talk about me joining the team because he's so busy with the Pipe contest. Then he said that if it weren't for Sid Barrow, Butch would have a lock on the title. That's when I mentioned meeting Wayne at the gym. When I started talking about what Wayne could do to Barrow for the right amount of money I thought he was going to freak out but he just listened. Then he asked me about Wayne — how well I know him, where he's from, that kind of stuff. He said he's going to think about the idea and he'd let me know. He asked me not to tell anyone about our conversation."

"Sounds like things went about as well as we could expect. The fact that he heard you out and is even considering the proposal is a good sign. I think we've got a shot."

"I kept expecting him to tell me I was talking crazy, maybe even kick me out of the PAB. But he didn't act that way at all. He actually looked like he was really seriously considering the idea. This whole thing is really weird for me."

"I know, and I really appreciate your help, Makua. We dangled some pretty good-looking bait under his nose; I just hope we can get him to take the hook. He's under pressure with the contest starting tomorrow so hopefully we won't have to wait too long for his answer."

"I can't help feeling guilty, like I'm tricking the guy into doing something wrong."

"No, you're doing a good thing. This guy has got to be stopped, look at all the people he's hurt so far. We're just exposing him for what he really is. All he had to do is say no and walk away."

"Yeah, Titus is telling me the same thing. So now we just wait?"

"That's all we can do. Remember, not a word to anyone and let me know as soon as you hear from Woods."

With Makua settled for now, a little voice in my head suddenly grew loud: "What the hell! You're standing on the beach at the world famous Banzai Pipeline. Go surf!"

During my last two trips to Hawaii, I didn't surf Pipe so even if I didn't catch one wave I would at least, get a fresh up close and personal look at the famous break. I also had a refrain from a stupid little saying from my childhood running through my head: "When in doubt, paddle out."

As I paddled, I could clearly remember magic days of catching epic waves. The crowds in the water were getting extreme and the odds of a "hoale" like me catching a good wave at Pipe are practically zero so it looked like my memories were going to have to last me but I had to give it my best shot. People work years to gain enough respect to be given a place in the pecking order so there were only two approaches that would work — I could either sit wide of the pack and try for a wave that occasionally shifts down past the regular takeoff area or I could sit out farther and west of the pack for the occasional wave that sometimes breaks in that area. Option number two seemed like the better plan since the swell was building rapidly and was now double overhead, which meant outside waves would be more frequent.

The pack of surfers at the main peak was dense and I recognized and said hello to several of the visiting pros. Both Josh and Barrow were in the lineup. My credibility got a big boost when I saw Tiger Esperanza and he gave me a high-five.

After a while, I ended up quite a distance from the main takeoff area. I positioned myself using a lineup based on a house on the beach that I had used successfully at other Pipe surf sessions and then I settled in to wait. Two hours later, I was still waiting. I tried to maintain my position and to not let my mind wander. Several quality waves had come through and been grabbed off by guys sitting near me. I paddled for, and missed, another giant peak that shifted away from me at the last possible second. Then, a group of three waves approached and I saw the first wave actually feather a bit on the second reef which meant that for the first time today, there were waves coming in with some size. The few people around me who were in the right spot started going for the first wave of the set. I paddled up the wave's face and over the top.

The decision to go on a wave or paddle over has to be made in a matter of seconds. It's a decision based on reading the conditions combined with pure instinct and luck. Surfing is a reflection of life. You ask yourself, "Do I take the wave that's here now or do I gamble and wait because there is a chance that the next wave will be better?"

I've lost track of the number of times I've gambled and lost, ending up with no wave at all and asking myself, "Why didn't I take that last wave? I could have had it, it was mine."

And then there are the times when the gamble pays off big, like pulling the lever of that one-armed bandit and coming up with triple acorns, bells and whistles.

I made the decision to gamble once again and paddled over the second wave of the set. This left me looking at a perfect 12-foot A-frame that had my name written all over it. It's difficult to describe the feelings that can occur in the few moments spent waiting as a wave rolls towards its inevitable conclusion after crossing thousands of miles to arrive at this point. It's so hard to sit still, you feel like jumping out of your skin — like a kid waking up Christmas morning and realizing that the best present ever is waiting under the tree. You are actually going to be given this beautiful wave to ride — nobody else, just you.

For some reason, I had a hard time getting into the wave but, after a two-hour wait I was not going to let this one get away. I just managed to paddle in under the bump at the top and suddenly I was free-falling down the vertical face. My inside rail grabbed as I hit the bottom and I could see the line I needed to take written on the face of the wave. I looked up at the huge lip throwing out over my head as I got deeper and deeper until it seemed impossible for me to escape. Then, a blast of spray hit me in the back and I was catapulted out onto the shoulder.

If I had been in Southern California, I would have been screaming and raising my fist in the air, claiming the wave for all I was worth but this was Pipe. I just wiped the water out of my eyes, did a cutback and bellied it out to the beach. Today, for once, I quit while I was ahead.

The current took me quite a way down the beach before I managed to wash up on shore. Several famous surfers own houses at Pipeline. A few of the other beachfront properties are owned by multinational clothing companies. As I walked by the first house along the pathway, I heard someone calling my name. There, seated on the first floor deck was Paul Maguire and Ellie. Sitting next to them, with his cast up on the railing, was Bobby Contraras. Several surf team members and photographers were standing around. I made my way over to Paul, feeling a little disappointed that nobody said anything about my wave.

Paul and Bobby had just arrived from the airport and were eager for a situation update. We went inside the house so we could talk in private. I told them that Makua had talked to Woods and that we were now waiting for Woods to make a decision.

"It sounds like Makua did a real good job in the way he brought up the subject. He made it out like he was just trying to help his Hawaiians win."

As usual, Paul had something to say. "This plan of yours sure involves a lot of waiting — waiting for word from Indo, now waiting for Woods. I just hope the waiting pays off."

Ellie slung an arm over Paul's shoulder. "You know what they say about all good things come to those who wait. I'm feeling pretty good about it. If Woods wasn't interested, he would have just told Makua to get lost."

Bobby turned to me. "Paul's been giving me updates but I want to hear from you on this, Mike: Why did these guys set me up?"

"Woods and Patel want Butch Chu to win the title this year so you had to be taken out of commission because with you out and Chu in, Woods sells millions in clothes and Patel cashes in on the publicity of the world's number-one surfer being a member of the PAB. The popularity of the Brotherhood spreads among the surfing community and its fans and its membership increases. It sounds like a pretty lame reason to kill and maim people but that's the truth as we know it so far."

Bobby poked at his cast with disgust. "Dude, surfing is supposed to be about having fun and enjoying nature not making money and power moves for religions."

Paul sat down next to Bobby. "If everything works out like we hope, both these guys will be prosecuted. Woods's business will be ruined and Patel will lose his position with The Brotherhood."

Bobby's a tough little nut. He had to be, growing up in the barrio with no father and surrounded by local gangs. I've personally seen him challenge a guy two heads taller than him. But when he spoke again, he had tears in his eyes. "You're talking about ruining their reputations and destroying their business. But Ramon is dead. My life has fallen apart. And nobody even knows what really happened to Arrington."

Bobby was right. There wasn't much any of us could say except that these guys deserved a much worse punishment.

"I promise we'll do everything we can. Let's give the plan a chance and see how things play out. Don't get down, man. You're going to be back and in the water ripping in no time and better than ever. Just hang in there. "

"Don't get me wrong, guys, I'm grateful. I guess I still can't believe that all this has really happened and what makes it worse is I can't remember hardly anything about Mexico. It's my fault because I couldn't stay away from drugs and alcohol and partying."

Ellie decided to speak up. "It's a hard lesson you had to learn Bobby, but now there's no going back. You can only go forward. You've got your family, your friends and the team behind you. Nobody's giving up on you so don't give up on yourself. I guarantee that this time next year you'll be number one on the team."

Now I knew why Ellie was the team manager. It was like all the tension had been let out of the room as she reached over and gave Bobby a big hug.

"And besides, if nothing else works we still have our secret weapon," I said, struggling to keep a serious expression.

"What secret weapon?" Bobby asked as Ellie continued her hug.

"Wayne."

Bobby broke into a big smile and Paul and Ellie started laughing. I was making a joke but seriously, if all else failed Wayne could be the weapon of last resort.

I asked Paul if we should get the police involved in this stage of our plan.

"Every time I've reached out to the police on this thing they've been a day late and a dollar short. Let's get Woods on tape first and then we'll make a decision."

As our group walked back out on to the porch, I finally couldn't help myself and asked Bobby if he'd seen my wave.

Standing there on his crutches he looked kind of blank. "No. Weren't you surfing down the beach?"

Damn. That wave was one of the best and heaviest, most life-threatening rides of my life and nobody saw it.

Then Bobby cracked up and everyone around me started laughing, too. I should have known — nothing that happens at this break goes unnoticed. I was even promised pictures by several of the photographers.

I practically sprinted back to the car to retrieve my cell phone but I didn't have any messages. I walked back to the beach house, grabbed a cold drink, scrounged up a chair and joined the assembled fans. Hanging out on the porch and watching classic Pipe peel off with some of the world's best surfers in the water was first-class entertainment but always in the back of my mind I was waiting for my cell phone to ring.

There was no doubt now the contest was definitely on for tomorrow. Some people around me grumbled that they should have started it today. It was certainly good enough contest conditions. With the contest starting, Woods was running out of time and I hoped this would force him to make a move.

Chapter 14

THE STING IS ON

Makua finally called at 3:00 p.m. Woods wanted to meet with him. In fact Woods had instructed Makua to come by his office to pick up cash and the keys to a company car so he could then go into town and rent a suite at the Waikiki Honolulu Arms Hotel. Makua was supposed to bring his friend, the hit man, to the hotel room at 9:00 p.m.

I told Makua to go ahead into town, rent the room and, if possible, to make sure there was an adjacent room available for me. We would keep in touch by phone. I poured out the soda I'd been nursing and gave Paul, Bobby, and Ellie the thumbs-up sign. "The meeting with our guy is set for nine tonight. I've got to go get things organized. Wish me luck."

As I walked down the beach, I could see that the contest preparations were nearly complete. All the tents and scaffolding were in place for the big event. I got Wayne on the phone and gave him the time of the meeting and location. "I'll come into town as soon I update Blakely. Start thinking like a hit man."

Blakely was working on all his electronic gear under a large tent. I had to be careful of what I said since there were people everywhere. "You know that meeting we've been trying to set up? It's set. Tonight at nine at the Waikiki Honolulu Arms Hotel."

"That's fine, gives me plenty of time to finish up here. I'm just testing and making adjustments now, anyhow. I'm glad it's tonight because once the contest starts it will be real tough for me to get away."

I motioned him over to a more private area of the tent. "I'll keep in touch by cell phone. Makua is renting the room so access won't be a problem."

"Good thing it's going to be inside. I'll finish up here and be there as soon as I can."

"I'm heading into town now. I'll call you with the room number as soon as I have it. I'm going to try to rent an adjoining room."

"The closer the better, but you'll be surprised about the operating range of some of this remote equipment."

When I arrived at the hotel, Wayne was waiting in the lobby. He was dressed in a T-shirt and shorts, like any other Waikiki tourist, but that slightly manic look in his eyes coupled with his bulging biceps and imposing height, gave him the look of someone deserving of a cautious respect.

Makua had booked room #804 under the name Henry Charles so I checked into room #805 and then we went up to see Makua. The suite included a sitting area with sliding glass doors to a small ocean-view balcony, a kitchenette and an adjoining bedroom and bathroom. The layout of Room #805 mirrored #804, with the sitting rooms on either side of the shared wall.

Makua seemed pleased that he successfully completed his part of the operation and I made sure he knew I appreciated his good work, even going so far as to offer him a reward. "Thanks, man, but I'll pass on that. I just wanted to see the right thing done."

Blakely called at 4:45 p.m. to say he was pulling into the hotel parking garage. I gave him the room numbers and started describing the layout as I had no idea how he was going to set-up.

"All my equipment is remote so microphones can go almost anywhere. Placing the cameras will be the hard part."

Blakely arrived carrying a laptop and a small suitcase. He placed the case on the coffee table and popped it open. Inside were several different foam-padded compartments filled with odd-shaped electronic instruments.

After the introductions were completed, we all agreed that the conversation between Wayne and Woods would most likely take place exactly in the area where we were sitting, the couch with two easy chairs across from it and a coffee table in the middle.

Blakely held up a device no bigger than a throat lozenge. "First, the mics."

He planted microphones behind the drapes and under the chairs as well under a cabinet in the kitchenette and under the desk near the sliding doors.

Then he began looking for camera locations, which, of course, was much harder. I made a quick trip down to the gift shop and brought back a vase of flowers that I placed on the kitchenette counter. It took some time to get it positioned correctly but Blakely finally got the camera-in-the-flower-arrangement setup working to his satisfaction. He insisted on placing a back-up camera. Our options were limited but Wayne suggested using the valance area at the top upper corner of the sliding glass door drapes. This placement necessitated a small hole be made in the fabric but it provided a nice birds-eye view of the sitting area.

Next, Blakely took his monitoring equipment to the adjoining room. While the rest of us sat around the coffee table and discussed the cover story Wayne and Makua would use during the meeting, Blakely went back and forth between the two rooms to make adjustments to his equipment.

"Okay, I'm as ready as I'll ever be," he announced. "Now all we need is for the star of the show to arrive."

Wayne, Blakely and I moved to the next room while Makua watched TV and dozed. Why should he worry? He had already done what he had been asked to do.

Wayne and I went over some basic stuff once more. Wayne was supposed to be a hard-ass ready to take anybody out in exchange for $10,000. Not necessarily kill them, but inflict serious damage. Wayne would want $5,000 up front and the rest when the job was done. Wayne was supposed to be leaving to go back to the mainland so he should appear to be worried about receiving his final payment when the job was done.

Time dragged by. Finally, I felt like I had to get out of the room so I decided to take my old standard beach walk from Ala Moana to Waikiki. My beach walk is something I try to do on every trip to Oahu. I started taking the walk when it was about the only form of entertainment that I could afford. Checking out the girls, as well as the hordes of tourists, is very entertaining and it keeps me in touch with the hustle and bustle of Honolulu. There are also many great surf spots spread along the five-mile stretch that offer some fun surf at certain times of the year when the North Shore can go flat for weeks at a time.

It was well after dark when I arrived back at the room. I could see from Blakely's monitor that Wayne and Makua had gotten a deck of cards and were playing penny ante poker while the TV droned in the background. Blakely was comfortably reading what looked like an electronic trade magazine but would periodically shoot a nervous look at his wristwatch, betraying that the waiting was starting to get to him. I attempted some small talk just to try to relieve some of the tension that was starting to become hard to ignore.

It was now ten after nine and no sign of Woods. At quarter after, Makua called Woods, who said he was having trouble parking but would be right up. By now, the tension was so bad I could have chewed my fingernails off. Blakely and I were seated in front of the monitor when Makua finally got up to let Woods into the suite. There were the usual introductions and handshakes, only no last names were given. An awkward silence followed as Woods walked around aimlessly and then disappeared into the bedroom. He returned to the sitting area and then walked over to the kitchenette. "Nice flowers."

Blakely started muttering under his breathe and nervously clenching and unclenching his fists.

"Compliments of the hotel," Makua said.

Woods leaned on the counter and touched the vase as he took a closer look at the lilies. My heart jumped into my mouth. His touch shifted the vase's position on the counter. He moved it back. When he pulled away, our camera view from that lens was pointed towards the wall.

Blakely cursed.

"But our overhead shot is still working fine."

Woods went back to the coffee table area where Wayne and Makua were seated. "Would you mind lifting up your shirt?" he asked Wayne. "This is not the kind of thing I do every day so I hope you understand if I'm a little nervous."

"Not a problem." Wayne lifted up his shirt and did a 360-degree turn.

Woods turned to Makua. "Why don't you go out for a short walk? I'll call you when Wayne and I are done here."

He was taking no chances.

After Makua left, Woods sat down across from Wayne. "I understand you need a job done on one of the contest surfers out on the North Shore?"

The moment of truth had arrived. This was the make-or-break point and Woods seemed reluctant to answer. After a long pause, he responded. "It's very important that the Hawaiian surfer, Butch Chu, win the contest. I want the Australian surfer Sid Barrow hurt so he will not be able to compete. I want him injured so that it looks like an accident."

"That type of accident can be hard to arrange. What do you have in mind?"

"A mugging or maybe a car accident that would leave him with a broken arm or leg or maybe just a dislocated shoulder. Whatever you do it has to either look like an accident or a mugging. I don't want him permanently injured, just out of the contest."

"How much time do I have to get the job done?"

"Barrow is a top seed so there is no way he will surf until next weekend at the earliest. Makua said that this type of job was your specialty and that you're dependable. Can you do this?"

"Oh, I can do the job the way you want it done but it will be harder and take longer than I had planned. I'm supposed to be leaving the Islands first of the week."

"I'll increase your fee to $12,000. I'll give you $5,000 down and the balance will be delivered to you by Makua as soon as Barrow is scratched from the contest."

"Fair enough. When can I get the up front money to seal the deal?"

"I brought the cash with me. I'll have Makua hand it over after I leave. Just remember I want a professional job. It has to be done soon and quietly with no mistakes. We won't talk or meet again. As a matter of fact, we've never met. I don't know you and you've never heard of me. Agreed?"

Wayne nodded. "Agreed."

"Makua will be the only person you will have any contact with. He can help you with the details of where Barrow is staying, what his schedule is like and his favorite surf spots. Any questions?"

Blakely began muttering under his breath again and I was sweating in an air-conditioned room. It was time to wrap this up. The longer they talked the better the chance that Wayne was going to slip up and make a mistake. But he delivered his next line like a soap opera pro.

"No questions. Don't worry, everything Makua has told you is true. I've been doing mixed martial arts all my life. You want somebody hurt; I'm the guy that can do it. Just remember this is a two-way street and I've got just as much to lose as you do. When the job is done, I want to be paid and on my way home the same day. No hold-ups or delays."

"You're speaking my language. We've got a deal." Woods reached over the coffee table and he and Wayne shook hands. "Wait here. I'll send Makua back with your money."

He got up and walked out the door and with that, the night's business was done and everyone got what they wanted — especially us. Blakely and I looked at each other with huge grins on our faces.

"I'm sure glad you wanted to place that second camera, that really saved our asses."

Blakely was too busy with his equipment to respond. He punched a key on his computer and turned the screen towards me, then stood back. The footage was remarkably clear and so was the sound. Our hit-man-for-hire sting operation was a resounding success.

Makua and Wayne came over waving a fat envelope containing $5,000 in cash. I called Paul and gave him the good news and agreed that we would all meet at the Pipe house as soon as we got things wrapped up at the hotel.

Later that night, we gathered at the beach house and watched our home movie. There was quite a bit of backslapping and congratulations going around and a great deal of the conversation centered on the best time and place to release the tape.

"Once that tape is made public Woods and his clothing business will be history," Ellie said. "He won't be able to sell a pair of flip-flops."

"Since all he cares about is the almighty dollar, that'll be so sweet," Bobby said. "But when the police see the tape won't they be able to prosecute the guy?"

Paul entered the discussion. "If you think about it logically then the answer to your question is yes. He's soliciting Wayne to attack somebody and money did change hands. But the police have been no help to us so far so I'd rather go with our original idea of exposing him on the web cast first and then get the police involved. I can't wait to see the look on his face when he sees the tape."

Blakely and I made eye contact because this was a subject we had already discussed. I let him take the lead.

"Mike and I talked about this and I have no doubt in my mind that when I show this tape to the web cast host tomorrow morning he will start drooling. This is the kind of thing these media types dream about. And the host, Steve Janner, can be a real bulldog once he gets his teeth into something. This is a once in a lifetime chance for him to turn the surfing world on its ear. I guarantee he'll grab the chance. This tape is solid gold."

"All right, Blakely, it's your baby." Paul pointed at him. "But don't blow it. We've all come too far to screw up now. And for God's sake take care of that tape."

"You don't have to worry about that Paul. I've already made two copies and have them stashed in separate locations."

We were all ready to call it a night. We had a very big day ahead of us. If all went as planned, our release of the video would inflict maximum public damage on Woods.

For convenience sake, Wayne spent the night at Paul's place. Ellie and I drove back to Dolphin Bay. By the time we hit the sack, it was close to 2:00 a.m. For once, my internal clock failed and the next morning Ellie had to wake me up. She was in full pre-contest team manager mode with a cup of coffee in one hand, a cell phone to her ear and out the door with a quick wave and barely a backwards glance. That was okay with me because I had my own fish to fry.

By the look of things out in the bay in the predawn light, there was a major swell and the contest would certainly start. I knew the narrow Kam Highway would be a mess of traffic and parking at the contest site would be scarce but I decided to drive anyway as there was a chance I would need the car.

As I walked up to the beach house, contest heats were already running in what looked like really good surf. The usual cast of characters was assembled on the deck. In the living room, Bobby and Wayne were watching the web cast on a big-screen TV.

"Well, look at who finally woke up," Wayne called as I walked into the house. "The great film producer decided to make an appearance."

"Someone's still on a high from his world-class performance last night, eh?"

I don't even think he heard me. "Blakely came by and whipped together this custom set-up for us. Now we get to watch the web cast on the big-screen with surround sound!"

"Not too shabby."

The web cast host, Steve Janner, a well-known fast-talking surfer about town, was on the big screen interviewing Sid Barrow, who was commenting on the unbelievable quality of the eight-to-10-feet waves. Barrow also expressed his relief at being seeded into the quarterfinals as it saved him from having to surf through the numerous elimination heats.

Paul walked in. "Morning. Mike, Blakely was by earlier and said Janner is on board and everything is looking good."

I took a walk down to the contest site. I was admitted, thanks to my White Sand team credentials, to the main tent area where the surfers prepare for their heats away from the milling crowds on the beach. The web cast area was in an adjoining tent. I could see Barrow and the host were still talking and doing commentary on the heat of surfers currently out in the water. It was a sight to behold; the clear blue sky as a backdrop for the top-to-bottom Pipeline screamers, the off-shore wind blowing the tops off the waves as the spectators "oh-ed" and "ah-ed" and the clusters of photographers behind their huge telephoto lenses clicked away like African big game hunters. The action at Pipe is usually close to the beach and the location combined with the waves' power and inside-out hollowness makes for an awesome contest venue.

I felt a nudge at my elbow. Blakely had materialized from amongst the crowd. "Sam Woods is in the house," he said quietly. "He'll be interviewed before the start of the fourth heat. I've gone over everything with Janner. He previewed the tape and the guy couldn't believe what he was seeing and hearing. We're really lucky Janner is such a ham. Somebody else might want to talk to the lawyers first. Not this guy, he can't wait to run the tape. He's looking forward to putting Woods in the cross hairs and I can tell he thinks it's going to make him famous."

"Good work. I'm going to check in at the house. I'll be back for the big moment."

On my walk back, I waved at a few people whom I recognized on the porches of some of the other beachfront properties. The Aussies were already in full party mode. They were probably still continuing from last night.

Paul, Bobby and Wayne were still the only people in the house who knew what was about to occur. I gave them the approximate time of the Woods interview as the web cast talking head host, Steve Janner, welcomed another prominent surfer to do a stint as guest commentator. I reminded Wayne, at a low volume, that we didn't know how Woods would react to being exposed. "As soon as they start the interview, you should head down to the tent area, just to make sure he doesn't get away."

Paul said he was going to watch the show with Bobby so I once again made my way down to the tent. As I entered, I noticed Ellie standing off to the side with Titus and Makua so I moved over in their direction and gave them an unobtrusive thumbs-up and pointed at my wrist to indicate that we were getting close.

Sam Woods was led to the interview area by one of the production assistants and once seated, Jennar introduced him to the multitudes viewing on the worldwide web. Janner asked his first question in an earnest and business-like manner: "What do you think Chu's chances are of clenching the title against the dark horses Josh Phillips and Pradratz and the point leader Barrow?"

"Chu does really well here at his home break. He's been surfing here since he was a little kid so I think his chances are excellent."

"Sam, I'm sure you've heard the rumor making the rounds, after the attack on Bobby Contraras and Clyde Arrington's death, that someone is trying to fix who wins the world's title this year. What's your opinion?"

"Well, Steve, I think that rumor is ridiculous. There are always people who are going to spread conspiracy theories. What we have here are two unrelated accidents."

I had to hand it to Janner — that was a good setup question designed to make Woods look even worse, if that was possible.

Janner continued in his deadpan announcer's voice. "Sam, I have a tape on the monitor I would like you to take a look at along with our viewers and give me any comments you'd care to make."

There, filling the monitor was our remarkably clear and audible hit man tape in all its glory. First, all the color drained from Woods's face, then his mouth dropped open as he heard himself on the tape: "I want Sid Barrow hurt so he will not be able to compete. I want him injured so that it looks like an accident."

All conversation in the tent ceased. The tape seemed incredibly loud amidst the silent crowd. The expression on Woods's face went from shock to stunned amazement and finally to blind panic. Janner was trying to prolong the interview and was halfway through his next question when Woods bolted from his chair. He didn't make it far. Woods ran straight into hit man Wayne, who grabbed his hand, stepped to the side and put him in an extremely uncomfortable looking "arm bar" hold. Our plan had been to return Woods to the beach house where we would wait with him until the police arrived. However, we had not planned on what happened next.

Wayne started walking Woods across the beach. Woods was bent forward at the waist with his arm elevated up and behind his back and was yelping in pain at every step. As the pair came into view of the Koala beach house, a mob of crazed Aussies started swarming out of the house pointing at Wayne and Woods. It was not hard to guess what was going to happen next so I calmly stepped in front of Woods holding my hands out in front in what I hoped was a calming gesture. The mob trampled me without even breaking stride.

Wayne was relieved of his prisoner but not without a fight. Several Australians went down before Wayne hit the sand, covered by a seething mass of screaming surfers. Sam Woods, meanwhile, was being systematically dismantled limb by limb. Then things got worse. Several members of Woods's surf team, who knew nothing about his recent web cast outing, came to his rescue. Soon, other locals joined in to help out their outnumbered "brahs" and the situation rapidly escalated into what can only be described as a full-scale beach riot.

The contest was shut down. Tourists ran for their lives. Roving packs of rioters attacked each other and ransacked the grandstands, concession areas and contest tents. I had no desire to be involved in a riot and once I was able to withdraw to the fringes, I spent considerable time trying to locate Woods but with no success. He had somehow managed to get away from his attackers and had vanished in the confusion. Black-clad riot police, complete with helmets, shields and batons were late in arriving because the narrow Kam highway was a traffic nightmare. Even I was unable to get Wayne back under control. Somehow, he had managed to become the de facto leader of the Australian mob, the ones who had originally attacked him. Wayne led his pack of Aussies on a sort of raid against the enemy Hawaiians who, they thought, had conspired to attack Sid Barrow. The beach resembled a scene from "Mad Max, Beyond The Thunderdome."

Paul, Bobby, Ellie and many other people were mesmerized by the riot, watching the violence from the safety of the deck. I reminded Paul that Woods was getting away and he should call the police. Bobby and I shook hands and I could tell by his beaming smile that he was very satisfied about ruining Woods's entire life.

Even with rioters running wild on the beach, I couldn't keep the stupid grin off my own face.

Wayne eventually calmed down and returned to the house. "Sorry I lost Woods, you guys, but there were just too many of them for me to handle."

He looked a little like a guilty dog expecting to be punished for his misdeeds. Paul came back outside. "I finally got through to the police, but because of the beach riot and all the confusion they don't know when they can have somebody out here to take a report. But we're on an island. It shouldn't be too hard to find Woods."

Bobby looked at me and then pointed out at the surf. "Mike, I know there's a lot going on but if I was you, I know where I'd be right now."

I grabbed my board and ran through the roving remnants of rioters down to the beach and paddled out into the emptiest Pipe lineup I have ever seen. The surf was still really good. Between waves, I watched the activity on the beach and it was quite lively. Eventually a line of riot police cleared the beach and then posted "Beach Closed" signs. Between the patrolling police and the beach closure, a dozen other guys and I had one of the world's best surf spots all to ourselves and since I would never in my lifetime have another chance like this, I intended to make the most of it. Everybody in the lineup realized what a freak occurrence uncrowded Pipeline waves were so there was none of the usual cut-throat tactics as people moved into the takeoff area in a somewhat orderly progression. After a couple of hours, I was even becoming more accustomed to the incredibly steep drops and constant threat of being caught out of position by a sneaker set because the swell was increasing relentlessly in size.

Occasionally, a surfer came down the path or popped out of the bushes only to be chased and marched off by the riot police. Even the people who resided in the beachfront properties were being refused access. Guys began going in as they became exhausted by the extreme conditions. This surf was not even in the same reality as the waves I usually surf so I began to conserve my energy and only went on waves on which I had a good chance of success. The brutal paddling conditions were starting to make my arms feel like lead. The sunlight was fading and there was only one other surfer still in the water when the biggest set of the day appeared like unbroken black lines, one after the other, all the way to the horizon as far as the eye could see. The approaching waves were starting to feather on the second reef and then I saw whitewater way outside on the third reef. There was no chance of paddling over this set. The other surfer was gone. He had picked off one of the first waves of the set. It was getting darker by the minute and I was alone, the only surfer still in the water at outside Pipeline. It had suddenly turned into a survival situation, so instead of paddling out, I started paddling over and in towards the beach. My only chance was to catch one of the next few waves. After that, I would be buried by tons of cascading whitewater as Pipe closed out from one end of the beach to the other.

I managed to paddle into a big thick wedge that was moving so fast away from me down the beach that by the time I jumped to my feet, the feeling was like being shot out of a cannon. The size of the wave was impossible to judge but as it hit the inside reef, it jacked up times two and started throwing a lip of water over my head that was so thick that when it landed over my outside shoulder, it sounded like one of those Honolulu pile drivers. I continued for as long as I could, feeling frozen in time and as insignificant as a bug that the ocean could squash at will.

Finally, at the last moment before the wave shut down, I dove in front and into the wave face, trying to penetrate the water as deeply as possible to escape the inevitable awesome power.

I clawed my way up through what seemed like miles of churning whitewater. The wave finally released me and I came to the surface, sputtering and coughing. My board was gone and I had time for a quick gulp of air before one giant wall of whitewater after another began relentlessly pushing and pounding me down the beach.

When I finally managed to pull myself up on the sand, I was all the way down almost to Pupukea and freaking out because I could not see my board anywhere on the beach. I started the trek back towards Pipe. Just about the time I should have been getting close to the beach house, I saw a flashlight beam up ahead moving side to side. It turned out to be a cop, still in full riot gear, and he had my beloved Magic Frye under his arm. He put my board down and I was preparing to be harassed but all he said was, "Well, brah, you certainly got your money's worth today."

I had been in the water for seven hours. Now that I had my board back, I started feeling relieved that I was alive and in one piece.

Chapter 15

HOME AGAIN

Wayne and I were on a plane back to the mainland the next morning; I had an appointment with a guy in a monastery. Back to the sleepy little beach town of Encinitas, where the odyssey had originally started, to finish up this business. Paul was still waiting to be interviewed by the police when we left for the airport. A pickup for questioning had been issued for Woods and the airports were on alert. Paul and I had agreed he would stay to handle the police and the pursuit of Woods because if they got a hold of me, I might not be allowed to leave the island.

The Pipe contest was on hold; the surf was just too big and besides it would take some time to repair the damage after the riot. The newsprint guy who was always hanging around broke the story for "The New York Times" and so our hit man tape was getting national exposure. Sam Woods and his company were decimated. It was just a matter of time before he was apprehended.

Wayne had weathered the riot with only a few scrapes and bruises to show for it and judging by the sound sleep he was enjoying, he was not the least bit worried about how to bring Mr. Harvey Patel to justice. What would my good friend Patel do now that his evil half-brother had been brought down? Would he run or sit tight and try to stonewall his way through? There was no hard evidence he had given the orders causing Ramon's death and Bobby's attack, only circumstantial evidence leading to a logical conclusion. Patel could blame the whole affair on Betet, who was now conveniently dead. I was sure that Patel would not walk blindly into a trap as Woods had. He probably suspected some of his secrets were out in the open and he would be on guard. I was also fairly certain Patel would not run. He had too much to lose — a position of power within the Brotherhood, a nice home and people in the community who looked up to him and admired him. The only thing I knew in my stubborn Irish soul was Patel was going down just like his brother, but how was still the question.

These thoughts kept running through my head as the engine noise droned on. There had to be some way to get to him. I felt bits and pieces coalescing into the beginnings of a plan — "A plan, a plan, my kingdom for a plan" — maybe not a completely watertight plan but still a good enough beginning that I felt free to lean my chair back and to catch some well-deserved Zs.

The approach to the San Diego airport is from the east so the planes fly over the rural county areas and then pass over downtown to come in for landings. During the approach, I looked out the window and saw two huge billowing plumes of smoke spiraling up from the remote backcountry area of San Diego County. It was fire season once again. When most parts of the country are anticipating a visit from Santa Claus, in Southern California we often get a visit from Santa Ana — the gusting powerful winds that propel out-of-control brush fires across the landscape, devouring indiscriminately small nondescript cabins and huge mansions alike. Sometimes, only an opposing force of nature can stop them — the crashing waves of the Pacific Ocean. Fire and water: two of the primordial elements of the universe battling it out, each victorious in its own realm while mankind stands by, a helpless spectator. Whether these firestorm disasters are related to climate change no one can say for certain, but they seem to be occurring with more frequency and ferocity and they have become a fact of life in Southern California.

The shuttle driver gave us the latest rundown on the fire situation. Tragically, people and homes had already been lost and nobody was even ready to hazard a guess as to when the fire would be contained. Wayne was, naturally, curious about what was going to happen next regarding Patel but I told him honestly that as yet I had no real plan and that I would call him as soon as I had something definite.

Wayne was dropped off first and then it was my turn. As we pulled up in front of the homestead, I noticed a strange car parked in front of my house. I had only been gone two weeks and the neighbors were already taking over my parking. Oh, the irritations of city living.

I opened the door with my usual "Hi honey, I'm home!" and was greeted with a crack on the back of my head.

I woke up to a strange groaning sound like an animal in pain. It took me a while to realize that I was the animal. I gently probed the area of bloody, sticky scalp at the back of my thankfully thick skull. I stopped groaning and pulled myself into a sitting position. Apparently, Patel was not content to sit idly by while I figured out our best plan of attack, and I had surprised someone looking for information. I made it to the couch and sat down, trying to remember where in the house I keep the aspirin. Later, I went room to room, holding a wet dishtowel to the back of my head, and surveyed the damage. The place had been ransacked, with particular attention paid to my once orderly office area. Drawers were pulled out, files dumped on the floor and my computer was turned on. The back door was open and the door jam was splintered.

My thought process was not working real well so I decided a trip to the emergency room was probably a good idea, but damned if I could remember where I had parked my truck so I was forced to go through the ordeal of getting the Jag out of the garage. Luckily, it started right up. The lady behind the desk at the emergency room took all my information, told me where to sit and cautioned me not to go to sleep since there was a chance I had received a concussion. My emergency room visit went surprisingly quickly, I was in and out in only six hours. I ended up with a shaved patch on my head, nine stitches, and several pokes in the ribs to keep me from going to sleep while I was waiting to be examined.

Waking up in the morning was more painful than usual. The back of my head was sore and tender and most surprising of all, it was almost 9:00 a.m. — way past my normal wake-up time. The first pot of coffee was almost gone before the phone rang. Paul Maguire was calling from the beach at Pipeline. No, Sam Woods had not been apprehended. Yes, Paul had been interviewed by a police detective. Yes, the contest was back underway. Now, it was my turn.

Even in my present fuzzy-headed condition, the plan, as far as I was concerned, was complete so I gave Paul the details. "I'm going to need you to call Harvey Patel and do your best to act really mad, maybe even a little irrational, so you're not making complete sense. Tell him the Honolulu Police have captured Sam Woods and that he has confessed to being Patel's half brother and is blaming Patel for everything in order to save himself. Don't forget the biggest bombshell. Tell him I personally went to the village where he, Woods and Betet grew up so we know he was giving the orders. Lay it on as thick as you like, we want this guy really worried because then he just might slip up and make a mistake."

"So, you want me to blame him for Ramon's and Arrington's deaths, the attack on Bobby, and the hiring of a hit man to go after Sid Barrow?"

"Yeah, hit him with everything. He won't know what we know for sure, especially if you tell him that Woods is saying he is the mastermind calling all the shots."

"You know, Mike, everything we have on Patel is circumstantial. It's not like with Woods where we had him cold. We can make Patel look really, really bad but without a confession, he's not going to go down."

"I know, the guy is either very good or very lucky. With Betet gone there's no direct connection to Bobby's attack or Ramon's or Arrington's deaths. The chances of Woods actually turning in his own brother are probably slim to none. This phone call idea is the only thing I can come up with to use against Patel and to be honest I'm really not expecting any earth-shattering results. But let's give it a shot and see what happens, maybe he'll panic and run, which would mean that at the very least, we destroyed his comfortable life and caused him to go into hiding. Then, we can leak the whole story to the media, which will definitely ruin his reputation. After that it might just be up to you go after him in civil court. You know, like they did with O.J. Simpson. They couldn't get him in criminal court but they nailed him big time in civil court."

"I'd like nothing better. And I know just the lawyer who can do it. So, when do I make this call?"

"The timing is critical. We need to get the most bang for our buck out of this call because we'll probably only get one shot at him. Wayne and I should be in a position to follow him; maybe he'll lead us to some hard evidence. But, I think we need to hold off for a while. Let me get a better handle on what's going on around here and then I'll let you know."

215

I got off the phone and started thinking. Patel did not know that we discovered the link between him and Woods so accordingly he did not know that we knew they were working together. Patel and Woods had undoubtedly talked after the beach riot, all Patel would know was that Woods had been caught trying to hire a hit man. This attempt to get at Patel could work because, with Woods supposedly in custody, Patel could not be 100-percent sure that Woods wouldn't throw him to the wolves to cut a deal and save himself. People who panic make mistakes; they run or try to destroy evidence that otherwise would probably remain undiscovered. The thought of Patel sitting comfortably within the confines of his compound irritated the hell out of me. I wanted to make him as miserable as possible.

I turned on the TV and found non-stop fire coverage on all the news channels. The offshore winds were gusting stronger and new fires, both from flying embers and firebugs, were flaring up all over the county. When I finally got around to opening the drapes on the front picture window I saw that the atmosphere outside was almost otherworldly. Ash particles were falling through a heavy gray pall of smoke-like fog and covering everything like a shroud. The newscasters were advising everyone to remain inside and to keep all doors and windows closed. The air quality was just about as bad as it could get.

My head was still not feeling all that great so I decided to stay at home, watch the fire news, and clean up the mess left by the break-in. I was also trying to figure out if there was anything Patel's people could have found in the house that could affect my current plan. After much consideration, I decided there was nothing to be found in the house that could be used against us, however, the break-in was an indication that Patel were getting desperate. Patel's people had broken into my house under cover of a residential burglary hoping to find out what I knew. He was getting nervous, no matter how careful Patel had been there was always that slim chance I had uncovered something that implicated him.

Sorting through the mail, I came across a city mailer. Patel's project, which had been denied by the Planning Commission, would be in front of the City Council for another hearing this week. Any type of bad press for Patel and the PAB's multi-million dollar mixed-use project would surely be denied; just one more chip in the pot that Patel stood to lose if his part in the plot was revealed. The articles and the broadcasts to date resulting from the Hawaii hit man tape had not mentioned a possible PAB connection. The entire complicated story was still not known.

I must have been cat-napping because the next thing I knew I was being awakened by a call from Paul. Woods had been taken into custody and was currently being questioned by the police. The time was right. Patel had to hear Woods was in custody from Paul.

"Paul, wait one hour to give me time to get out to the compound and then make the call. Give it your best shot."

"Don't worry, when I'm through with the guy he's going to think half the police force will be sitting on his door step with arrest warrants any minute. He'll want to pack his bags and run for the hills."

Wayne picked me up in his truck and we headed out to the Brotherhood compound to wait and see what actions Patel would take after the phone call from Paul.

As we traveled the narrow two-lane road, the smoke started to get thicker and we soon heard on the radio that another fire had developed. The new fire had already been given a name: The Sycamore Grove Fire. Having been through these firestorm situations before, I know that once the Fire Department's resources are depleted, they basically have no more equipment or personnel to send to new fire areas. The Sycamore Grove Fire would probably be left to burn until equipment and personnel became available.

We pulled into the large parking area outside the PAB compound. Cars were quickly leaving the lot. The wind and smoke indicated that the fire was headed directly for the compound. The instinct for self-preservation dictates that one should run from danger, which is what everyone was doing, but in a fire situation it's safer to seek shelter in the middle of a large open area than it is to try and negotiate a narrow tree-lined country road. Wayne and I parked in the middle of the empty lot to wait out the fire. My cell phone rang. Paul was on the line.

"I just got off the phone with Patel. I let him have it with both barrels. I even told him the Sheriffs were on their way with an arrest warrant. Naturally, he denied everything but I could tell he was plenty worried. He didn't really ask any questions and at the end pretty much hung up on me. Where are you guys ?"

"Wayne and I are parked in the visitor lot outside the compound gates. It looks like we have a major firestorm coming our way. Almost everybody has left the area. We're going to sit tight, it's too dangerous to try to leave right now."

"Well, unless there's a back entrance, Patel is still inside as of 10 minutes ago. Looks like he's going to stay put."

"You could be right. It would be suicide to try and leave now. If you don't hear from us in half an hour, send help."

As smoke and burning embers blew across the lot, it was hard to resist the urge to drive off in the truck. The fire was almost on top of us when a small compact car appeared at the compound gates and stopped. The driver was seemingly hesitant. I jumped out of the cab and started walking rapidly towards the gates. The car quickly accelerated past me. I saw Harvey Patel at the wheel, his eyes wide with panic. The car disappeared into a wall of smoke and there was no way we were going to follow.

The Sycamore Grove Fire consumed 8,000 acres, destroyed more than 100 homes, injured eight and killed five people. Patel was one of the casualties. His body was found the next day in the burnt-out shell of his car, his charred fingers still locked in a death grip on the steering wheel. Patel died in an inferno that had probably looked a lot like hell — a fitting end for such a supposedly religious person.

Wayne and I sat the fire out in the PAB compound parking lot. It passed us by quickly but the small brush fires and swirling smoke continued for hours. Eventually, the lot became a staging area for fire fighters and equipment. Once surrounded by fire trucks and personnel, we finally felt safe enough to relax.

EPILOGUE

Sid Barrow won the Pipe Pro and the world title with Pietro Pradratz second and Butch Chu third.

A couple of gringos in an off-road vehicle dropped off an envelope containing $5,000 to Ramon's relatives at their dusty little ranch house east of Ensenada. It was far from adequate in the way of compensation, but it was all we could do to try to ease the pain of his needless and unexplained death.

There would always be some unanswered questions. Patel was gone and Woods wasn't talking. Were they working alone or were other members of the Brotherhood involved? Why was Ramon killed? Had he been tricked into delivering Bobby to the deserted overlook and then changed his mind and tried to save Bobby? Or was his death just another ruthless example of the Brotherhood eliminating any links to their group? Did the PAB have anything to do with Arrington's death or was it just a tragic accident?

My daughter broke the entire story in the local paper and the story quickly went nationwide. The Peace and Atonement Brotherhood suffered a great deal of bad publicity but was eventually able to control the damage and is now as dynamic and powerful as ever. The group continues to send out clean-cut new members door to door.

Sam Woods's Third Reef Clothing Company never again opened its doors after the Pipeline beach riot. Woods skipped his bail and is still a fugitive but I have a feeling about where he can be found if it ever becomes necessary: in a small fishing village on the remote east coast of Bali.

Separately, Woods and Patel were probably not much different from your average man on the street, but together, one pushing the other, they could not resist the temptations of money, status and power. The opportunity presented itself and instead of passing it by and choosing the right path, they chose the path to their downfall and destruction. They serve as a reminder about how thin the dividing line between good and evil can be and how fate and circumstance sometimes conspire to cause men to cross that line.

Bobby Contraras was soon surfing again after a period if rehabilitation. But only time will tell if he'll ever make another run at the world title.

As for me, I recently received a letter from an old friend. He's in a Mexican prison and has asked for my help. The case seems interesting and I think I'll see what I can do for him. I don't plan to build any more houses, at least not for a while. I have taken quite a liking to my new career as The Surf Detective.